MURDER AT THE FOLLY

The Violet Carlyle Historical Mysteries

BETH BYERS

SUMMARY

September 1923

When Violet and Victor run into an old friend in Belgium, they have an idea of what to expect. What they don't expect is to be followed back to England, persuaded to spend an additional weekend away from home, or to have their group experience another murder.

This time, the suspect is their long-time friend Tomas St. Marks—a shell-shocked former soldier. The race is on to discover the real killer before someone they know to be gentle and kind is taken in for a crime he didn't commit.

For ReGina Welling. Your support has meant the world.

CHAPTER ONE

"Codswallop," Victor read with a chuckle, snapping the newspaper that had arrived from home and leaning back to relish the review. He even set down his cigarette, after a long drag, and cleared his throat before swallowing the rest of his cocktail. The glass clinked as he set it on the table next to him, and he grinned engagingly at his siblings, preparing to continue reading aloud.

Victor's hair was slicked back, and he was dapper in his pinstriped suit with a twinkle in his eye that said the best was yet to come. Both twins—Victor as well as Violet—were tall and slim, with pointed features and dark colouring. Violet was a bit paler, but she was far more careful about protecting herself from the sun. When adding in the powder she wore, she was several shades lighter than her brother. Her eyes were kohled, her lips red, her cheeks rouged, and her hair was longer, but they were clearly twins—male and female sides of the same coin.

"I object to everything about that story," Isolde sniffed. "I was never as dim as your ingénue. That you based your *Forsaken Virgin* on me is...is....too mean!"

"Darling, darling, darling," Violet said. "You were willing to marry a fat, old man who was nearly older than Father. You even knew Danvers had a mistress—a girl your own age—but it wasn't stopping you. You were downtrodden, sweet, *forsaken* one. Downtrodden, yes. Even still, darling, you were rather dim."

"Be nice," their oldest brother, Gerald, mildly scolded. He smiled at both of them and then reached out and touched Isolde's elbow as though to comfort her for her previous stupidity. "Continue, brother. I haven't read your tripe, but I wish to hear the review all the same."

"I thought we were being nice," Violet objected with a gasp.

"I'm not the one who wrote the review," Gerald said mildly, settling back in his chair and adjusting his shoulders. He waved his hand as if giving permission for Victor to continue reading the review of the twins' book, even steepling his fingers to prepare for the article.

Violet's gaze narrowed. "Yet, *brother dear,* you were the one to use the word *tripe*."

"Darling one," Gerald said, humoring her. "I am not the one who titled my story"—he deepened his voice—"*Forsaken Virgin Seduced by the Scarlet Ghost.* You should have been prepared for the words tripe and codswallop. Those might be the kindest words one could use."

Vi giggled, because she couldn't hear or say that title without laughing, and then tipped her glass at Victor. Then as one, the twins shot their older brother a furious, matching glance as if at daggers drawn. Only Lord Gerald Carlyle wasn't bothered.

Victor cleared his throat again. "Oh ho! Listen to this, love. 'No doubt the person behind this V. V. Twinnings is Victoria Violet, or some other such feminine persona, proving, yet again, that women should never have been taught to read, let alone write. Somewhere in the world today is a father who regrets not just teaching his child to read, but the far greater sin of allowing her to read novels. He has learned—too late—to repent. A regret I share having been forced to gag down this drivel.'"

Violet set down her glass with a precise click and crossed her arms over her chest. Her heel clicked against the floor as her rage exited through the steady tap, tap, tap of her foot.

"I still hate the story," Isolde said, glancing at the enraged Violet carefully. Lady Isolde Carlyle was younger than the twins, with a creaminess of complexion that matched her blonde hair and blue eyes. She was curvier than Violet as well as being the basis for the ingénue from the novel. "But surely the worst of the tripe is from you, Victor."

Violet snorted while Gerald poked at Isolde.

"What's this?" Victor asked. "You object to the story of a young Isla manipulated by conniving relatives into a marriage for money where she was abused and tortured, driven nearly mad? Whyever for, sweet one?"

The smirk on Gerald's face quite burned Violet's remaining rage. She giggled into her Negroni while Isolde's enraged gasp filled the air.

"I hate you all," she declared. "You are terrible, horrible, awful siblings!"

"We love you, little one. Wonderful news too, darling," Victor said to Isolde. "I have a note here from my friend, St. Marks. He's come to Bruges for the sea air or bright eyes. Your mother approves of his fortune. That should provide you comfort should you decide to throw yourself into his arms."

Isolde's gaze narrowed, as did Violet's. Vi knew all too well that the bright eyes in question were her own. She was also all too aware that Tomas St. Marks hadn't come to Bruges for Isolde or Victor, though the men were as close as brothers. Tomas had come for Violet.

Violet *wished* she could give her heart to him. She did love him, but only as she loved her brother, Gerald. Not as much as Victor, yet almost more than anyone else. Her heart, however, had left her. It was back in England with an oversized, handsome Detective Inspector. Tall and dashing, his severe jaw and penetrating eyes had seemed to peel away her layers and see the person behind Violet's cheery air. Let alone how his strong, large body made her feel small, something she'd become rather addicted to.

Isolde's mouth had dropped open, and she tried to hide her reaction by sipping her drink. She was too late and Victor crowed with triumph.

Victor's gaze turned to Violet despite the fact that he was teasing Isolde. Each twin knew the other better than they knew their own selves. No doubt he saw the flash of agony she felt, no doubt saw the desire to return home, no doubt saw how mentioning Tomas simply made her miss Jack even more.

Victor nodded to her the smallest bit. It was enough. She knew that meant he'd seen her storm of emotions and would do something to help.

"We've been invited to a party tomorrow, luvs. Tomas has taken some large monstrosity near here. We'll go. We'll dance, we'll drink, we'll eat something, Tomas will make eyes at our girls and you'll flutter your lashes and play coy as though you aren't calculating how many dresses his mountain of bullion will buy."

Violet kicked Victor, who smiled at her. He refilled her drink before topping his own. He didn't bother with Isolde, who rarely finished a drink since they'd come to Bruges, let alone Gerald, who was too boring for Negroni when there was bourbon present. The Negroni, after all, was made with genever, vermouth, Campari, and an orange peel. According to Gerald, bourbon was the drink of the ages. It drove Victor mad that Gerald could hardly be persuaded to a sip of the concoctions Victor created.

"What do you say we visit that little dress shop tomorrow?" Isolde asked Violet. "I have longing thoughts about that pale pink dress."

"I told you to buy it. It accents your colouring wonderfully," Violet said as she sipped from her cocktail glass, noting the smear of her lipstick and telling herself she'd need to reapply before they went dancing.

"Not that Vi objects to going shopping," Victor said. "How many more trunks do you need before we return home, beloved?"

"How many cases of genever and beer have you purchased?"

He winked in answer with a hand over his heart and a wounded expression before picking up his cigarette again.

"Mmm," Violet replied, "exactly my thoughts."

Gerald leaned back. "So are you two still writing tripe now that you have loads of the green?"

"Isla was born after our inheritance. Previous to Isla, we wrote the story of young Margaux the French orphan and the highwayman who loved her." Victor grinned at Gerald's shudder and added, "We couldn't leave your Isla where we did, Isolde. Soon, dearest one, you'll see Isla's next adventure, *Broken Surrender and the Scarlet Ghost.* Was the Scarlet Ghost truly a specter or perhaps Isla has an unknown champion? Return to Supernatural Tales to find out."

Gerald groaned while Violet laughed. It was possible *Broken Surrender* was an even more terrible title.

Victor crossed his legs. "I, for one, cannot wait to see what happens next with our intrepid ingénue."

"You're a fiend," Isolde wailed. She sniffed and then took Victor's cigarette. Isolde wasn't much of a smoker and the ill-thought-out drag made her cough until her tears were streaming.

Violet took the cigarette from Isolde. "Darling, go fix your makeup. I think we'll be leaving rather soon, won't we?"

"An auto will be here shortly," Victor said. "Dinner, dancing, drinks. A delightful time for all."

Isolde rose and went to fix her makeup. The moment she left the room, Victor faced Gerald. "We'll be going home next week, I think."

Gerald's brows rose. "I wasn't aware you were thinking of it, yet."

"Bruges is lovely." Victor leaned back, folding the newspaper. "But we never intended to stay here so long. Violet has business to conduct, I have business to pretend to conduct. We barely took up residence in my house before we left. It's past time, and we'd have long since left if not for Isolde being a bit of a clinger with Violet."

Gerald examined the twins. "Well, you said from the beginning that you weren't going to stay for our whole trip, and it has been most of the summer. I was thinking myself that we should consider somewhere warmer before the winter."

"Perhaps the Cayman Islands or Cyprus if you wanted something warm," Violet suggested. "Those are both places I'd like to visit now that we have some of the ready money."

"No, no," Victor declared. "Monaco. It just rolls off your tongue and promises exotic fun, doesn't it?"

"You could come with us." Gerald's gaze was fixed on Violet with enough weight that she knew he was wondering if she wanted to go home to Jack Wakefield more than she wanted to see more of the world.

Violet laughed merrily, refusing to answer the unspoken question. "We might have left Father too long alone with Lady Eleanor."

"Or," Victor countered, "now that Father realizes the games she was playing, perhaps we haven't given her enough alone time."

"If we leave her too long," Gerald said softly, "she'll warp that little blighter Geoffrey even more."

"There's nothing to be done there," Victor said. "Our youngest brother will always be spoiled. He'll learn his place when the promises of his mother fail to come to fruition."

"And yet," Violet said, "regardless of Father and Lady Eleanor and even young Geoffrey, there are other needs to attend to."

Violet had many things to do, but the most pressing involved a baby. She had provided her villa on the Amalfi Coast to an expectant, unmarried mother and had promised to try to find a place for the baby. Vi needed to get back to London and look into the homes she'd had her man of business investigate. They needed someone who was kind enough to love the baby as though their own while also not being the type of person to take out the mistakes of the mother on the child.

It was rather all too common for the sins of the parents to be placed on the child. Violet wouldn't abide that for this baby. She was tempted to take the child in herself, but she was keeping that plan as a backup. Violet also needed to deal with business matters from her Aunt Agatha's investment concerns and check in on the young girls she'd taken under her wing when she'd been trying to find out about the crimes of Isolde's former-betrothed.

She'd been writing to Anna Mathers, who was going back to school soon and had spent the holidays with her expecting sister on the Amalfi Coast, but Violet had only heard what was happening with Ginny Heyer because their butler, Hargreaves, was keeping an eye on the child. An unacceptable set of circumstances. Ginny had helped Violet recover the kidnapped Isolde. Violet would be damned before the child fell back onto the streets. She'd been placed into a school in London but she didn't want to go. Violet could understand that all too well, but she wouldn't see the girl get sucked into crime when she could rise above. Not after Ginny had been so instrumental in saving Isolde.

It was only last December when Vi and Victor had gone to their aunt's home to spend time with her and she'd been murdered. In the end, the murderer had ended up in asylum and Violet had become disgustingly wealthy. Victor, on the other hand, had become enviably wealthy.

The twins had gone from Aunt Agatha's home to the Amalfi Coast and then to London, where they'd met the dastard who had been betrothed to their little sister, Isolde. During the attempt to stop the wedding, the fiend had been murdered. The twins had been involved in both murder investigations.

Those investigations had thrown Violet and Victor into the path of Jack Wakefield, a sometime investigator for Scotland Yard. Violet might just be head over heels. Her rational brain told her to slow down to be certain what she was feeling was love, while her heart screamed that she was well and truly gone in love. Both parts of her worried that he'd meet another woman while she took care of Isolde. The poor lamb had needed to leave London after the murder of her betrothed on her wedding day.

Violet pasted a smile on her face that Victor recognized as a lie. She bounced onto her feet and said, "I better just go powder my nose before we go dancing."

CHAPTER TWO

"Violet, darling," Tomas said, kissing her cheek. He had taken both of her hands when she arrived, squeezed them tightly for a moment before letting only one go. Tomas pulled her right hand through the crook in his elbow. "Come, meet all my friends."

She could feel him shaking slightly under her fingertips and guessed that he was having one of his poor days. "Tomas." Her tone was half-indulgent and half-scolding. She squeezed his arm tightly, letting him take refuge in her presence. She was an anchor for him, helping him to avoid memories from the trenches. He'd survived the Great War, but he hadn't done it unscathed. What he was thinking throwing a loud party like this, she did not understand.

Victor had parked the auto while they entered, and Violet had been forced to hunt through the crowd for Tomas while Gerald had taken one look at the cloud of smoke and the dapper men who eyed Isolde like a prize, and tucked her arm through his, escaping with her to the dance floor.

Tomas handed Violet a glass. "It's a Collins on that tray,

love. Is that all right? We can hunt up a waiter with champagne or another with G&Ts."

"This is lovely, Tomas." Violet referred both to her drink and the massive house he'd rented. "This canal house is just like a fairytale."

"It is supposed to be, I think. These Belgians are a fanciful lot. Have you seen the Church of our Lady yet?" Violet nodded, but his invitation was undeterred. "Surely, you'll go with me all the same, won't you? Catch up about the old days? Perhaps tomorrow?"

She knew she wasn't going to avoid what was coming, so she smiled merrily and said, "Of course, my *friend*. Seeing you again is always a trip back to our childhood. How many times did we race through the woods like changelings?"

"All of the wonderful days," Tomas said. "I used to think about the woods and our swimming hole every day in the trenches. I swore if I lived I'd swim every year in that hole."

Violet flinched inside, hating to think of him like that. "And did you swim this year?" she asked brightly.

"I did," he said, with a grin down at her. She saw him from their shared childhood. As he was only a year or two older than Victor and Violet, they'd spent many a summer day barefoot together. "I went in March. It was so cold. It felt good until I caught the sniffles. All bunged up and held captive in front of a fire. Woolen blanket, buckets of tea, handkerchiefs for days, poor Mrs. Newstone having to listen to me whine."

"Oh, poor you," Violet laughed. "You should have known better. Are you yet a boy?"

He grinned as he replied, "All man, love. All grown."

"Tommy," a thick Italian voice called, and Violet turned with him to meet the woman. Her voice was deep and a touch too loud. When Vi faced her, all she saw at first was dark brown curls floating wildly around an olive face. The woman was a curvaceous bundle swathed in scarlet and black with jet beads and black fringe. The deep vee on her dress showed off far more of her chest than Violet would have been comfortable with.

The woman slid her hand into Tomas's free arm. "Who is this scrawny thing? She makes me feel three times the size I am."

There was just enough of a shimmy on her shoulders to indicate that she felt Violet's small chest was something to bemoan, and enough of an edge in that too-loud, husky voice to tell Violet she was unwelcome by at least one of the two.

Violet smiled prettily and tilted her head. She winked at Tomas, who didn't seem to quite know what to do with the loud woman. The Italian was leaning into Tomas's space, and Violet could feel him stiffen under her hand.

Violet turned so that Tomas was pulled towards her and out of the woman's hands. "Violet Carlyle. Tomas is my dear friend."

"Odd," the Italian woman purred. "I've never heard him talk of you. I am Bettina Marino. No doubt you've heard him speak of me."

Violet smirked as she set her glass down on a tray and took a new one. "If you haven't heard of Vi and Vic, you must not know Tomas very well. Lovely to meet you, Bettina." Vi leaned in and whispered, "Oh dear. I fear your beauty mark has smeared." In a louder voice, Violet added, "Tomas, you must meet Isolde. She's all grown up. I must warn you, Lady Eleanor has decided you're rich enough for Isolde."

Tomas laughed. He was a bit serious when he added, "You know my feelings on the matter."

"Mmmm." She did indeed and knew that he'd hunted her down to once again throw his heart at her feet.

Violet and Tomas moved through the crowd and found Gerald and Isolde. The house was lit dimly, with waiters carrying trays of drinks and a jazz musician singing to the side.

"Tomas, really? A band? Where did all of these people come from?"

"Some are traveling with me," he said, with a flush to his cheeks. "Some the others met in the last few days. I was a bit under the weather, I'm afraid, before I was able to look up you and Vic and send a note round."

Violet smiled up at him, ignoring the heat in his gaze. There was too much going unsaid between them. Under the weather meant he'd descended into the memories again. She wished she could tell him it would be all right. She wasn't sure it would be.

The first time she'd seen him descend into the memories, he'd been curled up in the corner of his bedroom, wild-haired and wild-eyed, rocking back and forth and seeing things again and again that he should never have seen or experienced the first time.

If that weren't enough baggage between them, there had been how she'd sat down next to him, rubbed his back, and talked to him until he'd come back to himself and looked at her as his personal savior. She and Victor had stayed with Tomas for weeks while he'd pulled out of the memories and learned to apply a few techniques that seemed to work for him. Walks alone when the visions started, focusing on other memories. Pushing out the bad with other ones. Good ones. The two of them had picked some out together when she'd realized that talking about their childhood grounded him more than anything else.

She knew when her attempts at help had given him a measure of solace that the history of proposals between them would not stop. They had started half in jest when she'd turned ten years old. She wished there was a way to comfort him, to be able to kneel by his side and talk of swimming or running through the woods, without having to offer him the rest of her. What he needed, she thought, was new memories with another woman. Someone else who could whisper of the first time they'd realized they were in love, or their first kiss, or their wedding day. Someone who *wasn't* Violet Carlyle.

She wasn't convinced he loved her as he said he did. He loved her, certainly. But she felt sure he loved her as Tomas loved Victor. Tomas just wasn't capable of realizing that you could love a woman without being *in love* with her. He knew he loved her, he knew that she wasn't *his* sister, therefore she must be his wife. She'd make him miserable in the end.

An outcome he didn't see. Tomas needed someone sweet, someone who wanted to be the center of his world. Someone who wouldn't mind spending weeks on end in the country for the quiet. Someone who wanted to be his other half, to bear his children, to live for him. That wasn't Violet. Not for Tomas anyway.

She squeezed his arm. "It's too loud for you now, Tomas. Are you having a bad day?"

"They're rarer and rarer, Vi. But I did have bad dreams last night. I'm afraid they've chased me into today. No matter." He gave her the 'all is jolly-good' look, which she knew to be pure drivel.

She squeezed his arm again as they bypassed a couple who were dancing as though they had been born with a song in their hearts. Vi paused long enough to watch them, and the man lifted the woman, spinning her.

"That is Juliette and François Boutet. They are a brother and sister team of dancers. They...well, somehow I've become saddled with them. They are lovely to watch, though, aren't they?"

Violet lifted a brow as she faced him, ignoring the rest of his explanation. They had, no doubt, found their way into Tomas's pocket. They looked rather different and Violet would have doubted the claim they were siblings if she and Gerald didn't look like strangers as well. Oh Tomas and his hangers-on, the poor fool. "And Bettina Marino?" Violet purred the name the way the woman had.

Tomas's flush deepened and he stuttered without really speaking.

"Tomas," Violet told him seriously, "I am not your mother."

"Oh, I know that too well, darling. It's not like that, but Bettina would like it to be."

They had finally reached Gerald and Isolde in the corner. Two gentlemen were standing in front of them, and Vi couldn't see who they were until Tomas said, "Algie, look who I've found."

Violet froze as Algernon turned, and with him, Theodophilus Smythe-Hill. A flash of his hands digging into her shoulders, of him pulling her hair too hard, of the demand that he *wanted* her and what she desired was of little consequence. She remembered in an undesired rush the feeling of helplessness, of the realization of how much weaker she was than Theodophilus when he manhandled her.

"Lady Violet Carlyle." Theodophilus's sneer mocked her reaction as though she had been the one in the wrong.

Violet froze in the face of his mean eyes and too-strong hands. She tried to shake the ghost of him touching her, but she couldn't quite do it. Her gaze darted to Algie, who flushed, and to Gerald, who looked on, concerned. Her brother knew something was wrong with Violet, but she'd never spoken of what happened beyond the initial report to Victor.

She knew she was safe, and yet seeing him made her feel very unsafe indeed.

"Vi, are you all right?" Isolde asked, her gaze flicking over her older sister and a rare flash of protectiveness coming from the younger sister.

A moment later, Victor pulled her from Tomas from behind. Her twin came out of nowhere, somehow knowing she needed him. Wrapping an arm around her shoulders, he asked Theo silkily, "Did we need to have a repeat of our previous conversation, Theo?"

The undisguised threat in Victor's voice had both Gerald and Tomas turning in consternation to the twins. Most only knew Victor as a jolly spaniel—the veneer he wore over his inner lion.

Violet flushed as Theo shrugged, lips twitching. "Are you the king of Bruges then? You think you can control wherever I go?"

Violet realized she was trembling, which pushed Victor into an effervescent rage. Her twin nudged her towards Tomas and then took Theo by the lapels, slamming him into the wall. "I have told you to stay away from my sister."

"I'm supposed to avoid every party she attends?" Theo's sneer belied what he'd done to her and Victor pulled Theo away from the wall to slam him back into it.

"Yes," Victor growled. "Yes. You avoid her. She arrives, you leave. You don't speak to her. You don't look at her. You don't breathe the air she breathes, or by Jove, you won't need to breathe."

"Tomas," Theo appealed, glancing at the host of the party.

Gerald took a slow sip of his bourbon and declared, "I wouldn't have thought of you like this, little brother." The insinuation was pride, not consternation.

"Why does he need to stay away from you?" Tomas asked Violet, his gaze searching hers. He knew her well enough to see the upset despite her solemn face.

Violet shook her head. Her trembling aside, she couldn't allow Tomas the role of protector. She couldn't let him step in. She couldn't let him want or act in that role—not if she was going to convince him to find the woman he needed.

"Vi?" Tomas almost begged.

She shook her head again and set down her drink, turning to Isolde. "Come with me."

Violet held out a hand to Isolde, who left Gerald and

tucked her arm through Vi's. The sight of Vi's shaking hand had Victor pulling Theo from the wall and hauling him towards the front door to throw him out.

Violet pulled Isolde into the water closet and leaned back against the wall. She took in a deep breath, let it out slowly, and then took in another and another.

Isolde, bless her, took Vi's hand without saying a word and didn't let go. Vi counted each breath, in long and slow, out even slower. One, two, three. She hadn't expected to see Theo again. Four, five, six. She hadn't expected to have to face him.

Seven. Bloody hell. Eight. A shaky breath that nearly ended in tears. Violet had thought that Victor had gotten rid of Theo. That Victor had scared Theo enough. A shaky, shaky breath. Nine.

Seeing him again was more than she had thought it would be. She had thought she'd moved on, but the memory was almost worse than the initial assault. In the moment, she'd been focused. Now she felt like an idiot. She knew it hadn't been as bad for her as it was for others. She knew she had been lucky. And yet, she could still feel the ghost of his fingers pressing into her shoulders and the horror of what had happened all at once.

It took her a few minutes to stand upright again. Isolde's eyes were fixed on Violet, but neither of the sisters said a word as Violet reeled her reactions in and placed them in a box. Both had been manhandled. Both had experienced the realization that should the struggle happen—they'd lose. Neither of them needed to discuss what happened. Violet ran cool water over the back of her hands until she stopped shaking and then powdered her nose, freshened her lipstick, and said with a bright smile, "I think a G&T is just the thing."

CHAPTER THREE

"I thought we might walk," Tomas said. "Though if you wish..."

"I'd love to walk," Violet replied. She was wearing a black dress that floated around her knees. It had accents of white at the shoulders, a tie at the neck and around her waist, making her waist seem lower than it was. The whole effect lengthened Violet into a slim stretch of femininity. She wouldn't wear gloves with a friend like Tomas. The seams rubbing along the sides of her fingers drove her mad, and she didn't need to stand on ceremony with a man she'd once been a grubby urchin with.

It was a fine enough day that she wouldn't need her knitted wool cape, but she took her hat and pinned it into place before turning to Tomas with a bright smile. Victor watched it all from the doorway of the library. He had said nothing when she'd returned to the party the previous evening, but she'd noted his bruised knuckles. The lion in her brother had come out once again, and Vi regretted her weakness being the cause of it.

He hadn't stopped watching her carefully, and Violet knew

if anyone else were taking her out, Victor would have found a reason to accompany them. Even Gerald, Violet thought. She gave Victor a smile and a wink, but his expression said he didn't believe it. He shouldn't. It was as much of a lie as the grin she tossed Tomas.

She knew it wasn't her fault that she was weaker than Theo, but she wished she had the strength to give him the pounding he deserved rather than having to leave it to Vic. At least with Victor, it was *almost* as if she'd done it herself.

"Be safe now." Victor knew what was coming as well as Violet, so the commiserating glance that followed was just for Violet.

The rooms the siblings had rented were on the canals as well. Tomas and Violet would be able to wind through the old city, arm in arm, talking of the old days while Tomas geared up to ask Violet to marry him once again.

They could see the bell tower and were aimed towards the Church of Our Lady as they walked along the canals whenever the route allowed it. The woven bricks of the road as they made their way towards the church were astoundingly lovely. Bruges may have just been the most beautiful city that Violet had ever seen.

"I've missed you," Tomas said. There was a bit of weight in his voice.

"And I rather missed you," Violet said brightly. Her hand was on the crook of his elbow, and he kept her tight to him, so they were brushing against each other as they walked.

"Life isn't what we'd thought it would be, is it?" He sounded solemn as they took in the beauty, the sun reflecting off of the water, the details of gorgeous stone mason work in the city.

Violet laughed merrily. "We were clever children, but stupid all the same. I believe we intended to have endless jam tarts, always get up with the sunrise, and never nap again. I took a nap just yesterday, and it was *delightful.*"

"Oh look," Tomas said, pointing to a little chocolate shop. "Remember how we used to filch chocolates from your aunt?"

Vi nodded, suddenly missing Aunt Agatha fiercely. The loss had gone from nearly unthought of to deep and abiding in a breath, and Violet's gaze glistened with the pain of it. By the heavens, how Violet wished she could curl up in her aunt's lap and tell her all that had happened. Those last days had been tinged by suspicion and worry. And when Aunt Agatha's life had been stolen, they didn't get their final goodbyes. It wasn't fair, and on occasion, Violet felt her body couldn't contain the combination of grief and fury. Little, however, about life was fair.

"Let's get some, shall we?"

Violet and Tomas walked into the little shop and a few minutes later left with rather more chocolates than even their younger selves would have been able to eat. Tomas took a bite of one and handed her the rest. There was something so intimate in the sharing of the same sweet, she paused before she took it.

Moments like these, moments when she needed to replace her companion with Jack, had been teaching her that what she felt, irrational as it was, was love.

Tomas looked at her through those thick lashes she'd envied since her youngest days and the smile he gave her went right through her, since it was pain-filled enough to stagger a lesser man.

"I'm haunted, Vi."

She nodded. She knew the feeling. She could only imagine what it felt like for it to be more than brothers or an aunt that crept into her thoughts. For Tomas, it was scores of brothers. Faces blown to bits before him. The sounds of those last, rattling breaths. She squeezed his arm since there was nothing to be said.

"Everywhere I go is grey and dark. I hear the screams. I..."

Violet didn't tell him it would be okay. He didn't need to

be condescended to, and she wasn't a person who lied because it was easy.

"It's a nice day, isn't it?" he asked, after several minutes trying to shake off the ghosts. He tilted the bag of chocolates towards her.

Violet took one. She wasn't quite capable of speaking at that moment, so she bit into the gold-dusted creation instead.

"It's warm," he added. "The sun is shining on my face, and I cannot feel it. I feel nothing but the cold of the trenches. I am never warm, Vi. Never."

A tear slipped down her cheek, but she ignored it and squeezed his arm again.

"That's lessened when you're around."

Violet glanced away, closing her eyes, to hide the rush of feeling. The guilt that even though she loved him, when he asked her to marry him, she would say no.

He didn't add to that statement, so they walked on in quiet as they passed the Belgian people going about their lives in the market where they sold their wares. They worked and lived while Violet and Tomas walked through the streets, followed by ghosts that wouldn't leave them be.

The bells of the church rang and Tomas jumped, but his hand tightened on hers when she checked to see if he was all right, and he took in the sight of her tears for him before his jaw clenched. He said, "Tell me about Smythe-Hill."

Violet shook her head, without saying a word.

He didn't press, and the bell tower came ever closer. They walked over a stone bridge covered in greenery with tree branches hanging low.

"It's lovely here. Would that London was so perfect."

She felt the pressure of Tomas's wants and recalled Jack's face to give herself courage.

Tomas took a seat on the wall between the street and the canal. He patted the spot next to him. Violet sat slowly down, repeating the injunction to herself to be brave. The bell tower overlooked them; the sun was shining; it was possibly the most beautiful place she'd ever been. A perfect location for what was to come. Would that her companion was a different one.

"Vi," Tomas started. His gaze was heavy on her. "Vi..."

"There you are!" The brash Italian voice cut in and Violet leapt with sheer, unadulterated gratitude. Never had Tomas been closer to getting her to say yes when she wished to say no. Especially, surrounded as they were, by their ghosts.

"I thought you might head this way." Bettina grinned down into their faces, the brightness not reaching her eyes. "Oh! Chocolates. You do think of me so kindly."

Violet bit the inside of her mouth as Bettina took the bag from Tomas and then snuggled into his side. He was a brick wall next to her. Vi choked on a laugh. A slight squeak escaped, and Tomas knew her well enough to nudge her side.

She glanced up at him, lips twisted in the face of his agony and laughed. She couldn't stop it.

"Oh," Violet said, with a smirk. "How clever you are to find your quarry as you have."

Her shoulders were shaking with her silent giggles and Tomas grinned at her despite his irritation.

"Shall we see the Madonna then?" Bettina demanded. She stood, hauling Tomas to his feet and winding her arm through his. "Are you coming? Or did you wish to rest for longer? British women are so wilting, no?"

Tomas's agonized, unvoiced plea had Violet rising. She did not wish to marry him, but she'd be damned if she saw this grasper weasel her way into his life.

"I shall persevere," Violet declared, adjusting her hat and taking Tomas's other arm so that Bettina wasn't able to claim the victory.

Bettina shot Violet a furious glance and then turned to Tomas, chattering as he walked woodenly between the ladies.

It didn't take long to reach the church and find the marble statue of the Madonna and Child.

"Oh," Violet said. "I've seen her before, but she steals right into my soul. She's so lovely."

"You British don't understand Mary," Bettina declared loudly. "With your dry prayers and stolid little churches."

Violet didn't bother to reply. Michelangelo was a genius, and this piece of brilliance required a long look, lingering, and —preferably—silent. Bettina was already distracted, but Tomas was unmoved by her tugging. Violet ignored them both, staring at Mary.

"You would think," Violet told Tomas, "that marble eyes would be dead. But not hers."

Bettina scoffed and moved away while Violet stared at the mother and the beautiful babe at her knee. Mary made Violet desire a child of her own with a sudden fierceness. It was all the more powerful when the man at her side wanted to do nothing more than give her that child. It was not, however, Tomas's child that she imagined.

A curly headed version of Jack. Those penetrating eyes filled with Violet's mischief. What an adventure that would be!

Violet moved on, pausing again for quite a while to stare up at the arches and crosses. The church was one of the most beautiful on earth, she was sure.

"To be remembered like this, yes?" Bettina demanded at the gold-encrusted tombs of Charles the Bold and his daughter. "This gold, I should like it in my hair."

Violet smiled politely and moved on. They made their way back out of the church and along the canals with Bettina pressing her chest into Tomas's arm and Violet giggling under her breath.

When they reached the rooms her siblings had rented, Violet said, "Victor and I return to England soon."

Tomas glanced swiftly at Violet while Bettina said, "Oh.

Passing each other on our travels. It is too bad, no?" Her tone was, however, exultant.

"Vi," Tomas said, "I just got here."

"I know," Violet said, biting her lip. She felt terrible about that, and it was in her tone. "I'm sorry, Tomas. I must...I wrote you about the villa," Violet said. She knew he'd catch the reference to the expectant mother.

He nodded.

"It must be handled." The baby needed a home. A good one. Nothing else would do.

There was no arguing with the pressure of that clock and no delaying it. He nodded once again.

"When will you be leaving?"

"Victor was to get passage on a boat leaving the day after tomorrow. Isolde and Gerald are staying for a few more weeks before going to Monaco. I...I'm sorry, Tomas. I really am."

"Oh, let's go there, yes?" Bettina insisted of Tomas. "Monaco is just the place."

Tomas ignored her, his gaze searching Violet's. "There is much at home that draws your attention."

So he'd heard the rumors of the earl's daughter and the Detective Inspector? How did they always miss the fact that Jack investigated because he was good at it and not because he must? His former commander and longtime friend pulled Jack in when his skills were needed. That was all. How did they miss the fact that Jack was rich in his own right and had no more need to pursue Violet for her fortune than he did any woman? He was not a man who would marry a woman for her money, and yet that was the way the story was told.

Violet did not reply to the question in Tomas's gaze, but Bettina's gaze sharpened with curiosity. With a woman's clever intuition, she demanded, "There is a love back in England, yes? Someone who occupies your thoughts and your heart? This is good. You should marry and settle down.

Already you have lines under your eyes. Your bloom is fading. It does fade earlier with British women."

Violet smiled politely. "It was a lovely walk, Tomas. So... nice...to be hunted down by you, Bettina. Meeting you again has been a curious adventure."

Bettina flushed at the accurate insinuation, but her gaze was triumphant as she pressed her chest into Tomas's arm. If only Bettina could see the disgust on Tomas's face. Perhaps then, she would let Tomas be and turn her attention to a more likely quarry.

CHAPTER FOUR

Rain was pouring hard and fierce when their trunks were taken out of their rooms to be sent down to the ship on the morning of their departure. Of their servants, Beatrice was excited to go home and Giles seemed utterly indifferent.

"I shall miss you so," Isolde wailed into Violet's arms.

"Suddenly I am the world's best sister. Don't worry, dear one. Gerald will buy you gowns as well. We shall torture young Isla in our next story to ease the parting."

Isolde shot Violet a stifling glance. "Why do I like you?"

"Worship me, I think you mean," Violet countered. She broke away from Isolde and kissed Gerald's cheek. "Sally forth with the might of the kingdom behind you, dear one. You shall need it to lead about this one."

"Oh!" Isolde nearly stomped her foot before catching herself.

Violet handed her sister a box. "Open it later. I shall miss you."

"And I you." Isolde sniffled.

"Don't worry," Victor told their little sister, kissing her

cheek, "we shall send you the latest adventures of Isla. You can use them as a guide for your own."

"You are right. Parting with you eases with each passing moment," Isolde told them.

Victor's twitching lips made clear that she'd guessed their intent.

"Come, darling one," Victor said to Violet. "No doubt Beatrice and Giles have arranged things just so. We must board our vessel, throw ourselves into the journey. It shall only be a short one, but I am afraid I didn't pay much attention to our arrival location beyond the shores of home. We shall be going to Ramsgate. Perhaps we should take a drive through Wickhambreaux?"

Violet flushed, to his delight. Jack Wakefield had grown up there.

"It's rather closer to Tomas than I imagined," Victor said. "Do you think they knew each other?"

Violet shook her head. She had no idea and certainly wasn't going to ask either.

"And how did he take your no?"

Violet glanced at her brother who, like she, hated that Tomas was suffering and, like she, was helpless to fix it.

"He didn't get to ask," Violet admitted. "That Italian woman appeared rather like the destroying angel."

"Destroying or saving?" Victor asked.

The twins had discussed time and again Tomas's feelings, and more than once Victor had told her to be blunt. She felt she had been previously. She'd carefully laid down her thoughts, but Tomas couldn't accept them, so he set them aside and went back to hoping.

"He's so stubborn!"

"He is rather fixated on you. He always has been."

"He'd have stopped it by now if not for the war," Vi groaned, laying her head on Victor's shoulder.

"Many things would be different, sweet one, if not for the war."

The twins boarded the boat and as they did, they both froze as they heard Bettina Marino moan, "Darling, we just got to Belgium. Surely we could go to France instead? Or perhaps Liechtenstein? Venice is always lovely. Better than Bruges, yes? Let's go there."

At the top of the gangplank, they turned back to see Tomas, along with his slew of hangers-on and Bettina on his arm, pressing herself into his side.

Whatever Tomas's initial reply, it was drowned out by an, "Oh! Oh!"

Tomas had taken hold of Bettina. Violet wondered if he had finally gotten tired of Bettina plastering her body against his.

Tomas shouted, "Bettina! Go to Liechtenstein! Go to Venice! Go home to Florence! I am going none of those places!"

"You are chasing that English twig, and she doesn't want you, mio amore. She wants that yard man and there is nothing you can do about it. Everyone has heard of the earl's daughter and the yard man. Why chase the twig when she is for another? Am I not woman enough?" Her voice was shrill as she demanded, "More than enough?"

Violet gasped and Victor groaned, but they both stared in shock as Tomas shouted, "I don't want you! I have told you this. Were you not chasing poor Algie? Do you think I don't know you threw him over because you thought I had more money? What about Charles? I've seen you looking at him when you think I won't notice. Foolish woman, leave me be!"

Bettina brought forth tears and moaned into a ready handkerchief as Tomas pushed her from his arms to a very blond companion. "There, there," the man said, shooting a nasty glance towards Tomas, who'd stalked off.

The twins jumped down from the gangplank and hurried

forward before they'd have to interact with Tomas after that scene.

"Oh Victor," Violet said.

"He's not done trying, little love," Victor told her, wrapping his arm around her shoulders. "It seems your destroying angel didn't prevent yet another proposal, as they've chased us to the ship. Onward and forward, dear one."

"Let's go to our room, please? Before we have to pretend to have not heard that scene."

The journey was only a short one, but they'd taken a cabin for each of them. They'd arrive in Ramsgate during the night, and this way they could sleep comfortably and disembark in the morning. Violet threw her hat on a chair and herself on the bed, kicking off her shoes a moment later. The disarray bothered her, but she ignored it, curling up on the bed.

She had not slept well, haunted by dreams of both her ghosts and Tomas's. Everyone had been in pieces and no one had been happy. Blood seemed to bathe them until she thought she might drown in it.

Victor left Violet when Beatrice arrived a few minutes later. With the maid to man the door, Victor went to find Tomas, and Violet let sleep take her.

As evening approached, Violet dressed for dinner at the captain's table along with the other first class passengers. She wasn't feeling particularly bright or happy since her dreams had been no better during her nap than they'd been the night before. At least when she woke, her room was clean, Beatrice was mending stockings near the porthole, and there was both tea and sandwiches. Violet had Beatrice bring in the typewriter and writing desk, and Violet wiled the afternoon away by trying to make a list of business that needed to be completed soon after she got home.

Her dress was lovely, though; however, it *was* black. Black with sleeves that came just below her elbow, peeked through to her skin with black silk lining to cover the pertinent bits and black beads. She wore a set of long black jet beads.

"You, sweet one, need black pearls," Victor said as he held out his arm to her. "I think I'll get them for you. Our birthday is coming soon. I have a little something else in the works, of course. But it strikes me that black pearls are just the thing."

"Funny," Violet said merrily, "I was thinking I'd get you a cigarette. Just one. Or perhaps a new pair of wool socks. Or, I know, a little monkey. The kind that our grandmother carried around on her shoulder."

"You know that monkey bit me," Victor protested. "I still dream about that little beastie. He swings through my dreams, with my tin soldier in his grubby paw, laughing at me from the curtains."

Violet slowly grinned as Victor led her away from her cabin.

"I know you better than that. You've got something in the works for me. Practical, because you are the business-minded one. And I am the frivolous one who buys jewelry."

Violet shot him a look then mimicked him. "Actually, I think you mean I buy jewelry because it's easy. I remember your birthday because it's mine, dear sister. Then I walk over to some jewelry store, pick something out, and grin engagingly."

Victor laughed at her imitation. Then his tone turned careful. "I have news darling." Violet paused, turning back to him. He wore a blue suit with a blue and white striped shirt. His shoes shone in the light of the hallway, having been polished by the reliable Giles. His perfect veneer did not match the way he was not quite meeting her gaze.

Violet's expression was knowing. "What have you done?"

"You know that you're my favourite person, sweet one."

Violet cocked her head at Victor and raised a solitary brow.

"I can't say no to him," Victor pled. "Love me still, please."

Violet sighed. "What did you promise him?" She didn't need to know he referred to Tomas. There was really only Tomas when it came to people that Victor might be persuaded against what Violet might want—and even then—only if Victor was sure that Violet wouldn't truly object.

"A weekend. His house. Old times. But..." Victor tried an engaging grin. "Sweet one. Dear sister. Womb mate."

Violet smacked his arm and demanded, "Yes?"

"I thought perhaps a party would be in order. Tomas agreed."

Violet's brows rose. She did enjoy a good party, but in the middle of the countryside with no warning? She hardly thought the servants would thank them or that there would be friends enough for it to be notable.

"Tina! You must stop!"

The low husky, familiar laugh had Violet pulling Victor to a stop and pressing a finger over her lips. She winked lightly. The staircase that led to the deck was just ahead. Just behind it was the captain's dining hall.

On the other side of that staircase, out of the view of the twins but not out of hearing, was Bettina Marino and whoever she was...assaulting.

"What if I don't want to?" Bettina purred.

There were the sounds of a bit of a scuffle and a low, female chuckle.

Violet glanced up at Victor. That hadn't been Tomas. He knew, of course, that the woman who was throwing herself at him wasn't *just* throwing herself at him.

Violet thought back to that moment when they boarded the ship and made an internal bet that he did care, but only because his pride was bothered.

"Do you think I want you now?" the man demanded. "Do

you think I don't know you don't love me? You care only about....about....money!"

There was a low chuckle and a man's gasp and then Bettina said, "Darling, you know it's not like that. You know that security is important for both of us."

"Don't," the man growled.

"Can't I love you and find security too?"

"What? No! No! Of course not. He's my friend. Do you think I would betray him like that?"

Bettina murmured something too low to hear and there was the sound of a low laugh. A moment later a door beyond the staircase opened and the sounds of passengers gathering for dinner prompted Violet and Victor to step forward.

They entered the captain's dining room. Both twins looked a bit too eagerly around to see who might have been in the hall with Bettina, but whoever it had been, he'd already been absorbed by those attending. Bettina stood with her hand on Tomas's arm. He looked down at her in a sort of angry bafflement while the twins' cousin, Algernon, was accepting a cocktail from one of the crew. The blonde man from earlier who'd had Bettina shoved at him was standing near the door with a cocktail.

The captain stepped to the fore of the gathered diners and introduced himself. "I understand that many of you know each other."

Violet noted the dancers she had seen at Tomas's party and a couple she did not recognize who were talking with a ship's officer. Beyond them, there was also a single gentleman who was eyeing the ladies in the group as though picking out a horse.

Violet cleared her throat and allowed Victor to get a cocktail for them both.

"I believe we are waiting for one more," the captain said.

"Ah..." Algie replied. "Well...ah...Mr. Smythe-Hill sends his regrets."

Victor snorted under his breath and Tomas looked at Violet, searching for the answer she refused to give him. Violet hated the rush of horror she felt knowing Theodophilus was on the ship and the rush of relief that he wouldn't be at dinner.

The undercurrents in the room were salacious indeed, and Violet perked up as she looked around for a pending dustup. There was rather a lot more to be excited about. She was on her way back to England. If Jack hadn't found someone else, she could discover if she was well and truly in love. She'd be able to sleep in her own bed, not look after Isolde, take care of the worries about the girls—Anna and Ginny, as well as the coming baby who needed a home.

Violet had spent the afternoon journaling and making a list of things she needed to resolve as quickly as possible. She'd even written a telegram for her man of business, Mr. Fredericks, to set aside time for her next week. She did want to mosey back to London, but the things that needed to be done were pressing.

Too much responsibility, really, for a bright young thing. However, Vi thought, she *had* spent the last few months lying on boats in canals, eating chocolates, and shopping with her sister, with a few shorter trips to Luxembourg, Amsterdam, and Cologne.

Violet had ordered her brother a case of black current liqueur after a visit to Cologne, along with kirsch, German beer, and some honey wine from Luxembourg. She'd also sent Giles out specifically to gather as many cocktail recipes as he could while they were out. She had written them up in a little book for Victor and had been working on the collection of recipes almost since his last birthday. Would he really buy her black pearls? A strand of the kind that was fashionable at the moment would be expensive indeed, but she had to admit, she wanted one desperately now that he'd mentioned it.

"Whatever did you leave Bruges for London for?" Bettina

asked querulously of the twins, as the diners came together. "Don't you wish to travel?"

"We've been away from home since last Christmas," Victor said. "Except for a short trip back to London."

"That was when your sister murdered her fiancé, no? You got your paramour to pin it on the son, yes?" Bettina had a mean turn to her mouth as she smirked over at Violet and Victor.

The captain cleared his throat. "Ahh, perhaps—"

"No," Tomas argued furiously. "Isolde murdered no one. You know this. Everyone knows this. She was a victim of some...some...madman who thought he could take what he wanted from her. He murdered his own father to do it. And Vi does not have a paramour."

Violet was near rage when she deliberately ground out, "Lovely weather, isn't it?"

One of the ship's officers stared at her. "You must enjoy the rain."

"The scent and smell of rain is the way I know I'm home. There isn't much difference in weather, however, between Bruges and London. Don't you think it was why we were so comfortable there, Victor?"

"Indeed," he said and asked about a recent horse race that he'd read about.

CHAPTER FIVE

The ship docked while Violet was sleeping, but she rose early to the gentle tap-tap of her maid, Beatrice, at the door.

"Hello, luv," Violet greeted as she shoved back her eye mask and put on her kimono. Beatrice had brought Turkish coffee, toast, and fruit, and Violet moaned in delight.

"I thought you'd like that," Beatrice said. "The ship's doctor is a fan and insists on having it available for himself. When I found that they had it in the kitchens, Giles and I persuaded the cook to share."

"You are a cherub," Violet said merrily, breathing in the deep scent of her coffee. "Did you use your fine eyes and a bright smile, or did Giles bribe them?"

Beatrice grinned and admitted, "A little of both, my lady. Miss Violet, Mr. Giles says we'll be staying in Kent for a few days. Did you want me to transfer any of your luggage?"

"I fear we'll be a bit of a mess until we're back home. Just do your best, and I promise not to throw any hairbrushes at you."

Beatrice laughed and opened Violet's trunks to pull out a dress for the day. "Did you want the blue?"

"With this rain, I think it must be the grey."

She sipped her coffee while Beatrice worked, wondering how the coming days would turn out. She knew the proposal was coming her way. She would have to try, once again, to persuade him to look beyond her. Another explanation of why she wasn't going to marry him. How? How to make him believe that she loved him only as a brother?

Violet could imagine it so clearly. Maybe she should just tell him. Something along the lines of, 'I am even more certain now, Tomas. Now that I've met Jack. He might not love me, but I love him.'

If she said that, would he accept it or would he just keep on asking? Hoping? Looking at her with those desperate eyes?

Would he point out that she didn't even know if Jack loved her? If Tomas understood that, would it be enough that Jack occupied Violet's thoughts? That when Violet danced in Jack's arms, she felt more alive than at any other time? That she preferred his company—even to Victor's? Victor, who Violet needed like she needed to breathe?

"It will be nice to be back in London, my lady. With Mrs. Lila and Miss Gwennie and your own house. Are you looking forward to it?"

"Oh, yes," Violet said, smiling serenely and sipping the deep, dark coffee. It wasn't Lila and Gwennie that she was both terrified and excited to see again.

"My lady..."

Violet glanced up at the tentative voice. "Yes?"

"It's..." Beatrice glanced around, avoiding Violet's gaze and then added, "Mr. Theo is..."

"He's with Algernon," Violet said carefully.

Beatrice glanced at Violet. "I believe they've been traveling together with Mr. St. Marks, and I'm concerned Mr. Theo will be at the next house. I can sleep in your room. Whatever you need."

Violet smiled and rose, cupping Beatrice's cheek and dropping a kiss onto her forehead. "You really are a cherub, and there is no way that Victor will allow Theodophilus Smythe-Hill in the same house as me."

"His man is almost as smarmy as he is, my lady." Beatrice shuddered.

"You be careful, my love," Violet said, "and remember, we are on your side. Not his."

Violet rose. They'd be disembarking soon. She put on the reasonable grey wool dress. At least it had a drop waist. Violet added sensible shoes with a bit of a sigh.

She slowly did her makeup, lining her eyes, as she nibbled toast and listened to Beatrice chatter about going home. Beatrice, it seemed, had something of an infatuation for the footman three doors down and wondered if he was yet available or if some other girl had snapped him up.

It was a trouble that Violet could understand all too well. She carefully applied a bright red lip to counteract the grey reasonableness of her dress and then helped Beatrice to gather up all the little things. Violet knew that Beatrice was careful, but Victor spent even more time lingering over his dress than Violet, so Vi might as well help. They'd be waiting for a while to disembark.

Violet sipped a second cup of coffee, putting her journal and a pen in her bag, along with her newest pulp magazine and the latest Tarzan novel. She hoped that Victor had taken an auto for them, so they wouldn't be dependent upon Tomas for every escape from his house. He'd happily share a vehicle with them, he'd just also accompany them. Not an issue if they were picking up typing paper or ribbons or some of that goop that Victor put in his hair, but more of a problem if they wanted to pry into Jack's childhood.

Violet arranged her traveling writing desk and another thought occurred to her. The memory of the last time they'd returned home and being teased. She tapped her fingers against her palm for a moment and then wrote out a quick note for Hargreaves. She would have Beatrice post it as soon as possible. The twins' birthday was coming quickly, and Victor spoiled her dreadfully. She wanted to win this year.

Victor tapped at her door as Violet put on her cloche and Beatrice took the last of Violet's things out of the cabin. She took one glance around and then wound her arm around Victor's.

"Will we have our own auto?" Violet asked.

He grinned down at her. "Feeling the grasping hands of love already, darling?"

"You know I care for Tomas," she struggled to say amid the conflicting emotions. She shrugged, helpless to elaborate.

Victor squeezed her hand. "I know. If we cared less about him, we could cut ties."

"But we *do* care about him."

"Eventually your Jack will persuade you or drag you to the altar, and Tomas will give up on the idea of you. Then, he'll look wider and realize how poorly you two would fit."

Violet sniffed and then Victor pulled her back to stop her. The other set of siblings, the French dancers, were arguing ahead, and they paused to give them space. Neither of the duo seemed to realize they had an audience as the sister looked up at her brother, placing a hand on his lapel and leaning into his space. Whatever she whispered was frantic and her brother scoffed and shoved her, pushing ahead and leaving her alone in the hall.

Victor tugged Violet into movement as the French woman looked up, saw them, and pretended to smile before rushing back into her cabin.

"Shall we go slowly to the house, love?"

Violet considered it. "Are they all going to Tomas's house?"

"All but Theo." Victor growled a little in the back of his throat before he said, "Shall I kill him for you? Or sell him to a trader in the East? Press him into servitude? Send him to the mines?"

Violet laughed though neither of them were amused, and they stepped out into the drizzle. Beatrice was ready with an umbrella and they hurried down the gangplank and to the car. By the time they reached it, Violet had stepped into three puddles and been soaked up to her knees, despite the umbrella, sensible shoes, and her coat. Violet suggested, "Perhaps instead, we shall go to our rooms at Tomas's house and dry out?"

"Good choice, darling one," Victor said.

Tomas's home was one of those big brick rectangles with rolling lawns and even a tower folly in the large expanse of the verdant grass. The butler was ready at the door as they walked up the steps, and the look on his face was harried and revealed his thoughts: could he have had more time than a telegram a day or two before they all arrived?

"Mr. Hull," Violet said, happily. "How is your mother? Is she feeling better? I'm so sorry to cast our wet selves on your good nature."

The poor fellow grinned at them with a strained sort of happiness and sent them up to their rooms after taking their wet coats. By the time Violet had removed her shoes, soaked stockings, and her hat, a housemaid had been in to light a fire, and Beatrice had appeared with a trunk and dry clothes. Violet disregarded all of the dresses for pajamas, thick wool socks, and her favourite kimono.

The housekeeper appeared soon after with tea and a greeting, and Violet kissed the woman's cheeks. "Beatrice, darling, give Mrs. Newstone one of the boxes of chocolates we brought back."

"Oh, thank you, my lady!"

Violet winked at the housekeeper who took the box gratefully and left a moment later.

Violet sighed into the tea and slowly stretched her legs

out towards the fire to warm her feet. She had gotten too cold on the walk from the ship to the auto.

"Mr. Victor sent you this, my lady," Beatrice said, handing Violet a stack of paper that had been tied with a piece of twine. It was the last pass of their next book. She would read over his changes and then they'd start the next one. Violet already had some ideas. They might be centered around a clingy Italian fortune hunter. She found the more books she wrote the more her current thoughts found their way to the page. Even if it was just an excess of chocolates and scenes on canals like the story in her hands, or the Italian woman that just may die in the next book.

"Dear," Violet said to Beatrice, who was sorting Violet's dresses and hanging them in the armoire. "Would you be so good as to have the typewriter brought into my room?"

She decided to write in her journal for a few minutes on her bed, snuggled under the blankets. Her words were mostly a jumble, repeating herself as she tried way after way in the pages to explain her state of mind to Tomas without hurting him. She'd paced too much of the previous night trying to figure out how to end things with him in a way that he would accept.

She'd journaled about all of her worries—especially Jack—as she tried to discover her thoughts through her writing, but she'd still come up without a response. It wasn't like she hadn't said 'no' before—she had. Each and every time. It wasn't like she hadn't said she didn't love Tomas the way that he wanted before. If anything, being around Tomas after being around Jack had shown her that her instincts were right. Tomas lived in the same part of her heart as Gerald and Isolde. Whereas Jack had made his own place, right in the center.

By Jove, she thought in awe, she *had* fallen in love with him. How had this happened? And what had happened to being young and modern? To taking control of her life? Would marrying him take that from her?

Her soul cried out immediately an answer she didn't expect—no. Not with Jack. Maybe with someone like Algie or Tomas who expected to be the center of their spouse's life—but not Jack. He knew her too well. Far too well for that.

CHAPTER SIX

Violet had changed from her kimono after her nap since she expected someone would show up at her room sooner or later, and she'd have to join the others for luncheon. It was well-thought too, since Beatrice answered a knock on Violet's bedroom door just as Violet was settling into her ingénue's newest story. Violet felt that a heroine this dim needed to be scared a little more before setting her free to her happy ending. Isla was the right heroine for the time she'd been created, back when Violet was bemoaning Isolde's idiocy and lack of will. But now that Isolde had been rescued and Violet didn't see her sister as quite so stupid, it seemed like a good time to create someone new.

Violet looked up from her typewriter to see Tomas standing in her doorway. She hadn't seen him that morning when they'd left the ship or when they'd arrived to his house. This was the first time he'd had her alone since Bettina scuppered his proposal. He looked down, staring at his feet before he asked, "Would you walk with me?"

She could see that his ghosts were hovering again, and she wished she could shoo them away. Her heart leapt into her throat as she examined his face. He had that intent look about him. Gone was the boy she'd known—her second brother—back was the man who wanted something from her she couldn't give. It was a combination of stubborn and nervous.

Her answer belied all of her actual thoughts when she answered, "Always."

She promised to meet him in the great hall in a few minutes. Beatrice handed Violet her shoes as she ran a brush through her hair, updated her lipstick. She was dressed in one of her more sensible dresses, a navy sailor kind of dress. Violet added woolen stockings instead of silk ones and her second favourite pair of sensible shoes since her first were still drying out. The chill from the earlier drizzle hadn't quite fled, but warm, dry stockings would help that. She decided upon her knitted wool cape and her cloche.

In minutes, they left the house. She could have lingered, but she wanted this over with even though she had no idea how to convey her feelings. The rain had stopped, but the chill was still present. Violet put her hand on Tomas's arm but didn't let him pull her close. The angle of her body was all attention without the intimacy he was trying to create. The problem, of course, was that they knew each other far too well for that.

He noted her position, the slight stiffness when he tried to pull her closer, and a frown crossed his face. "He's not here."

Violet blinked. She had no idea who he was talking about. Then she remembered that Theodophilus Smythe-Hill had been on the ship returning to England with the rest of them. What had happened? Had Victor done something that prevented his arrival at Tomas's home? Violet was suddenly certain that her twin had done just that.

She licked her lips quickly and let Tomas pull her a little

closer. The shock of what must have happened had loosened her defenses.

"I wish you would tell me," he started.

She shook her head.

"Why?" He was nearly desperate.

Violet decided that enough was enough. Maybe she needed to stop being kind.

"Tomas," she said, and he started to answer, but she cut him off. "I can't let you take care of me."

"Why?" Tomas demanded. "What is so wrong with that? Haven't we cared for each other since we were children?" He stopped and took her gently by the shoulders. Did he know how he was echoing Theodophilus on that dark day? Both men wanted something from her she had no desire to give. "Why is it so wrong to want to protect you?"

"You know why. You want me to let you take care of me."

"And is that so bad?" He sounded hurt, and she felt guilty for it. The guilt caused by *his* feelings was chased by her own anger.

"Yes!" Violet said hotly. Theo had wanted something she didn't want to give. Tomas wanted the same. Neither seemed willing to accept her 'no.'

She pulled away. The difference between the men was vast, but too narrow for her at the moment. She shook her head, reminding herself that Tomas was her lifelong friend. When she spoke, it was gently. "If you wanted to protect and love me as another brother, I would tell you everything. I would do that because I love you and trust you like I do my *brothers*. Tomas, I know you are going to propose."

He didn't say anything. His jaw clenched and his familiar, handsome face was both hurt and angry.

"I wish I could tell you that I loved you the way that you want me to."

He started to speak.

Violet held up a hand and continued, "But I don't, and

to be honest, when you asked when we were young blighters, I thought it was all a joke. I am tired of this tension between us. I'm tired of people assuming that because I am female, I don't know what I want. I *do* know what I want. The only people who give me the credit of knowing my own mind are Victor and—to my endless surprise—Father."

"Vi..." Tomas cupped her cheek as he stared at her. "Why won't you let me try? Why won't you try back? Am I so repellant?"

She stepped back. "When I lost Aunt Agatha, I realized what her life was like. She'd lost her husband. She spent her days creating a future for a progeny that weren't her own. She...Tomas..."

"She loved you like her own child," Tomas said, clearly not understanding.

Violet knew she wasn't making sense. Her thoughts about that were all jumbled up in her grief and loss and the guilt that she hadn't been able to stop Aunt Agatha's murder.

Tomas continued. "Raising and loving and creating something for you wasn't emptiness. Do you think Aunt Agatha was unhappy being a second mother to you?"

"No," Violet said simply. "No, but the life she wanted didn't pan out for her, Tomas. She had to create a new one when fate took away what she wanted, a new life that melded what she loved from her old life and what was available to her after losing her husband."

"What does that have to do with you and me?"

"What you want is *not* available to you," Violet told him. "Accept it."

He seemed utterly shocked. "I don't understand why you won't give me a chance. You must hate me."

Violet laughed. "You know I don't. I'm not going to be your wife, Tomas. No matter how many times you ask. No matter how much I care about you."

"I only feel like myself when you're around." He sounded almost broken, desperate.

"I love another, Tomas. He might love me. He might not, but either way, I can't...I won't...pretend to love you. Not as a wife. Not when I don't."

That had been the right combination of words. Finally, she thought he believed her. He also looked as though she'd taken away all the colour in his world.

Tomas nodded, pale. "I understand."

"If you'd let me be your sister..."

"I don't know if I can do that. I don't know that any man would understand that. If this fellow loves you back...he won't want me around."

"I can't be what you need. I can't be your wife. I would be your sister. Jack..."

"I don't want you to leave me." The truth outed a moment later. "The ghosts leave when you're around."

His gaze searched her face, the tension thick and almost capable of smothering them. "I..."

A shriek pierced the air, high-pitched and feminine. It was followed by the sound of something breaking and then a long slew of curses. Violet and Tomas looked towards the house as one, the tension gone in the shock of the commotion.

Violet glanced at him, horrified by what was happening in his house. Then she laughed at the look of helplessness on his face.

A moment later his lips twitched. "Who'd have thought that this was what growing up was all about. Declined proposals. The horrors of war. Bad dreams, and the most terrible hangers-on."

"It's your fault, you bedamned blighter, letting that woman latch onto you."

He grinned at her and the boy from her childhood flashed in his eyes. "It's not just her. Those odd French dancers. Theodophilus, though I did tell him he was out."

"Don't know how to get rid of them?"

He nodded, a reluctant smile crossing his face.

"What if I do it for you? Her, those leeching siblings, even Algie."

"Then I'll be alone," he said, and nearly shuddered. "The silence is worse than when it gets too loud, Vi."

"Come on," she said, putting her arm through his and giving him a squeeze. "Vic and I would never leave you alone, Tomas."

His grip was too tight on her fingers as they walked back to the house.

"Who do you think she was shouting at this time?" Violet asked him.

He shrugged. "It could be any of them. I might be the only one she hasn't taken to her bosom. She's a viper. When it ends, it's never pretty."

Violet laughed as he blushed brilliantly.

"Darling one," Violet said, "do you think she'll turn to Victor before we get rid of her?"

"He is rich." A dawning light of utter joy crossed his face as he glanced around for eavesdroppers. "I'll drop that he recently inherited."

"Oh no," Violet said, "Let me do that. I want to see the look on his face."

Tomas's shout of laughter was just what she wanted. They went in only to immediately see Victor smoking in the library. At the sight of her twin, the two of them broke into contagious giggles that even had the clueless Victor smiling.

"Do you promise?" Tomas asked a moment later.

To get rid of Bettina? Yes. To not leave him alone. That too. Violet nodded.

"What are we promising?" Victor asked.

"Mischief," Violet declared lightly.

"You've asked Violet to conduct mischief for you?" Victor

asked, lighting another cigarette and handing it to Tomas. "You've found the right devil for that."

"I knew she was the one," Tomas joked as he took the cigarette, "when she told Bettina her birthmark had smeared."

Violet winked, curtsied, and fled. She had no doubt that Victor would draw out of Tomas what had happened and that Victor would appear sooner or later at her bedroom door.

"I called for reinforcements while you were out," Victor said from the doorway of her room.

Violet paused in her typing and looked up slowly, the specter and the virgin fading from her thoughts as she blinked stupidly at her brother. She ran a hand through her hair and asked, "Reinforcements?"

"Denny, Lila, Gwennie if they still have her."

Violet gasped.

"John Davies too. I thought I would do what I could for sweet Gwyneth."

Violet choked on her laugh. "Tomas flirts with Gwennie."

"He does indeed."

"John is the kind of man who gets a good push when he thinks someone else might sneak in and take what he thinks is his."

Victor chuckled. "How does matchmaker look on me?"

Violet sniffed and examined him through a pretend monocle. "Smashing, my good fellow, smashing!"

"Besides, I knew Tomas would propose. I knew you'd crush his heart. I knew you'd need a buffer. They'll be down on the afternoon train. I thought we might go for an adventure in the morning before they arrive, get them from the train on the way back, and secure ourselves against the ensuing drama. That Italian woman has had fury and spite in her eyes all day."

There was something in Victor's gaze that said she wasn't the only one up to mischief. Speaking of, Violet rang the bell for Beatrice, though who she really needed was Hull, the butler. All she said to the machinations of her brother was, "That sounds lovely."

He smirked at her and she looked impassively back at him.

"Dinner is soon, love. Should be exciting, yes?" He'd dropped into a terrible Italian accent with the last part.

"Go on with you. I must pretty up myself to be in the face of this goddess among women."

"You refer to the prying Bettina and the alluring Juliette? That Juliette is..."

Violet paused. "Has my brother succumbed to love?"

Victor grinned and shook his head as he replied with a wicked laugh. "Succumbed, no. Love was never what was being offered."

Violet snorted and shoved her brother out of her room.

CHAPTER SEVEN

Beatrice was sent for Hull, and Mrs. Newstone, the housekeeper, arrived a few minutes later.

Violet greeted them in her bedroom. "I am well aware that what I am about to say is very...different."

Both of the servants looked at Violet without expression. There was the light of interest in their otherwise impassive gazes.

"I am not the lady of this house, nor will I be."

There was enough of a reaction on Mrs. Newstone's lined face that Violet was aware that the housekeeper, at least, had guessed Tomas's feelings.

"I am assured, however, that you both care for Mr. St. Marks as much as I do. I am certain that you wish for his happiness as much as do I. And I am sure that I can count on you for your discretion."

They both nodded.

"Bettina Marino and the French dancers are hangers-on who Mr. St. Marks is too kind to rid himself of."

The servants were stone-faced.

"I am uncertain of Mr. Charles Stroud; however, I would be unsurprised if he too is taking advantage of Mr. St. Marks."

They couldn't reply to such a declaration, but Violet didn't need them to reply. They all knew each other rather well.

"This will be resolved. I know you are very, very good at your work and this household is run like a tight ship, well organized, well done in every part. Mr. St. Marks would be lost without you."

"Thank you, my lady," Mrs. Newstone said, and Mr. Hull nodded.

"That ends now," Violet told them mischievously, "as far as those three go. I'll consider upon Mr. Stroud. I know they've been friends for some time, but I won't have him making Tomas worse by pushing him into loud parties and such."

"I believe Mr. Stroud is a friend from before the war, my lady," Mr. Hull said. "Mr. St. Marks was happy when he arrived."

"Lovely. We have our targets. Cold tea. Fires that don't get lit. Dresses don't get pressed. Whatever little irritations we can ensure will remove the comfort of this house. Let me be utterly clear. Bettina Marino intends to be the mistress of this house, and it is an outcome that we will not allow."

Mrs. Newstone's lips twitched and she carefully said, "I'm not sure that small discomforts in the face of Mr. St. Marks's deep pockets will be enough."

"Worry not," Violet declared merrily. "This is but our opening salvo. If it comes to it, Victor and I will simply take Mr. St. Marks with us to our house in London and not extend the invitation beyond him. Once that occurs, the house will be shut up so you may enjoy a holiday by the sea, at our expense, of course. We shall scold Mr. St. Marks into avoiding further ill-thought-out invitations and be done with it."

Violet grinned and winked. "Well now... I believe it is time to dress for dinner and, no doubt, I am interfering with your duties."

"And should complaints be made?" Mr. Hull asked.

"Apologize profusely, provide your regrets, and carry on."

"Mr. St. Marks takes pride in this household," Mrs. Newstone stated.

"Help has been requested. Worry not. I will ensure that this does not affect you."

They left and Violet drew herself a bath. While she washed, Beatrice laid out Vi's long, nude dress. It floated above her ankles by about five inches, but in a way that seemed to indicate that there was layer upon layer of fabric. The dress was beaded with tiny gold beads and crystals that made it seem to flicker. Tomas was one for candles in his dining room despite modern lighting, so she'd twinkle with each movement of the flames.

Violet set aside her favourite long strand of pearls for a necklace that would lie delicately against her collarbones. It was a simple gold chain broken up by black flowers lined in gold. She wore matching ear bobs.

Violet placed a headband around her hair with a gold feather that popped up merrily over her ear. Violet considered and then added red lipstick to finish the look. She knew she looked lovely, but the truth was, Juliette Boutet would outshine most women even when they literally sparkled as Violet would in the candlelight.

No matter. Violet wasn't one to begrudge someone else the better looks.

"You look lovely, my lady," Beatrice declared.

Violet grinned. "Aren't you the sweetest girl?"

The dinner gong rang, and Violet winked and left the mess to Beatrice, who had become nearly as bothered by messes as Violet. She asked Beatrice to return her jewelry to the safe, and then she left her bedroom.

They had gathered outside of the dining room and Violet had missed the early drinks while she lingered over her makeup. She counted herself out of luck not for that but for the way Victor was sidestepping away from Juliette Boutet.

Tomas was doing a similar dance with Bettina. Violet smirked and her humour was caught by Charles Stroud, who winked at her as they watched. Violet stepped in, taking Tomas's arm and earning a nasty look from Victor for saving the other man.

"Miss Marino," Violet said glibly. "Don't you just look lovely."

"Why thank you. You glisten like a thousand gaudy jewels. This is the word, no?"

Violet grinned brightly. "I'm sure that is what you meant. Your hair is so lively. Tell me, is it always like that? Or do you use a special process to turn it into a cloud around your head?"

"Just good luck," Bettina growled.

"It is eye-catching, isn't it? Tomas, I think Victor and I shall have a big party for our birthday in London. You'll come and stay with us, of course."

Bettina's gaze narrowed on Violet as she continued, "Where will your travel take you next, Bettina? Home to Italy?" It was clear where Violet's hopes lay. It was also clear that Violet intended to take Tomas away from the woman. Take him away and also not take him for herself. Bettina's gaze was sheer murder. The invitation to the birthday party without extending the invite to Bettina had been rather rude, Violet thought with a twitch of her lips.

"We shall see," Bettina licked her lips and glanced up through her lashes at Tomas, clinging to his arm as she pressed her breasts into his side. The nature of her offer was clear. Tomas's answering blush was delightful.

Violet grinned, then said, "Oh look." She used the moment to tug Tomas free of Bettina. "It's Mr. Hull." Under her breath, she told Tomas, "Prepare yourself, darling, for complaints about the servants."

He started under her hand, and she winked at him. They entered the dining hall for the meal. Bettina was seated next to Algernon and Tomas. Algie glanced at her, scowled, and turned back to his plate.

Juliette was murmuring to Victor, who teased her back, but the look in his gaze was that of a gazelle being pursued by a lion.

Violet grinned at her brother when Juliette placed her hand on his wrist and said something to him so low, he had to lean towards her or cup his hands to his ear with a hearty, "Eh?"

The food was perfect for Violet, but she noted how the plates were set in front of the Boutets and Miss Marino. Bettina's plate was missing half the food. Miss Boutet received a bowl of soup with barely anything in it. She glanced down at it and ignored the bowl entirely as she cast out her lures towards Violet's twin.

When the dinner was finally over, the tips of Bettina's ears were red with irritation, and she'd gotten louder and louder as the evening went on. "Really, my love," she said to Tomas. "You should consider new staff. Your man quite neglected my wine glass."

"Did he?" Tomas asked blithely in a rather practiced way. "That doesn't seem quite right. I'll have to have a word with him."

He grinned at her charmingly and then crossed to the drink cart to make up drinks with Victor. Violet followed after them and told them both, "You look a bit piqued, dear ones. Is it that you've been turned into lambs for the slaughtering?"

Both men shot her irritated glances, but she ignored them. With a wink, she abandoned them as Juliette and

Bettina returned to the hunt. Violet took the G&T her brother had made her and a seat near the fire.

A moment later, Charles Stroud and Algernon joined her. "Abandoned by the ladies, my good fellows?"

"Don't be like that, cuz," Algie moaned. "Those females are cats."

"Mmm," Violet said, enjoying the way he squirmed. "Better than the jackal you've been consorting with."

Mr. Stroud glanced between them. "I think I shall have a cocktail myself."

"Why aren't you on my side, Vi?" Algie asked. "Theo is a friend. You are too hard on him."

"Why aren't you on mine, cousin?" Violet countered, sipping her cocktail. "You knew what Theo was when he connived to get you into debt to him. And you, dear cousin"—her address was wickedly sarcastic and she glanced him over without an ounce of understanding—"decided the easiest way out of your mess was to throw me to your wolf. If that wasn't bad enough, when you were rescued, you didn't shake him loose. Are you in debt to him again?"

"It wasn't like that," Algie whined. "Don't be like that. Theo's a good enough fellow. Maybe a bit—"

"Don't dress up your wolf as a sheep to me, Algie. Don't think we'll be friends as long as he's around. You, me, or Victor."

"Or it seems," Algie groaned, "Tomas. What is it that you do to make them worship you so? You're pretty enough, and I suppose Victor has been saddled with you so long he couldn't imagine anything else, but Tomas?"

"I've known Tomas almost as long as you, Algie. And I always liked him better than you. He was less of a worm."

Algie shot her a wounded look. "You're the cat. At least with Tina you know what you want."

Violet waved her cousin away, only instead he leaned back

quizzically. "So what about it? Shall we wed? Free your brother of your weight. I'll take it on."

Violet laughed in his face before realizing he was serious. "Is this how you propose? Insult someone and then act as though your *hand* were a favour? You have an eye on my money."

"So? You never should have gotten it all."

"Is that what your snake, Theo, has been whispering in your ear?"

"And if it is?"

Violet sipped her cocktail lazily. "You need better friends," she suggested. "I will never, ever wed you."

Algie's laugh was a little nasty. "Do you think that your father will let you marry Wakefield?"

"I don't have to marry anyone. It's a new world, cousin. One where I don't have to ask my father who to marry and one where I don't have to marry at all. That means you, Tomas, Theo, even Jack. You're looking at a freed bird, not a cat."

CHAPTER EIGHT

The sound of Bettina shrieking pulled Violet from her story the next morning. She cast a nasty look towards the room Bettina was using and then walked to the window. The weather was clear with the look of a crisp, cool day.

Violet chose a light beige dress with cream stitching that formed embroidered dragons along the sleeves and the drop waist. She straightened the lines of her silk stockings, placed dark brown t-strap shoes on her feet, and buckled them into place before putting her brown fur-trimmed coat over the top.

Bettina's door was open when Violet passed and she could see Bettina shouting at Algie. A part of Violet was absolutely fine with leaving the idiot in the fangs of the viper, but he *was* an idiot. Violet could remember his grief at losing Aunt Agatha too. She could remember him as a duffer of a child who'd chased after her and Victor, always wanting to be a part of things. She could remember him offering her a blueberry tart with a grin and a wink.

"Algernon," Violet said, "I need your assistance, please."

"You! You get out of here," Bettina hissed. "You get out of

here. You wicked thing! You ruin everything! What have you done? You show up. Tomas doesn't look at me the same anymore. Charles acts as though I'm venomous. It's all you, no? The scarlet temptress."

Violet hid, her grin at the new title of her next book. Thank you very much, Miss Marino, Violet thought. "I suspect," Violet said idly, "it is the way that you throw yourself from the bird in hand to the next richest fellow available. Algernon would have successfully made a good husband. He's affable, easily led, and he'll end up with a good income since his father has repented and turned his business around. You won't be part of that now, though, because Algie is aware of your fickle, avaricious heart."

Victor stepped out of his room and watched Violet save Algernon with a bit of a smile about his lips.

Violet hid her sudden evil delight as she added, "I don't know Mr. Stroud, but he seems like a man who isn't so interested in the woman who threw him over. Tomas will never, ever succumb to a woman as loud as you. His mother might be Spanish, but Tomas is pure British in his feeling, and you, my dear, are simply too brazen. You must be stauncher. More...stolid to pull Tomas's attention."

Bettina gaped like a fish with Algernon staring on in shock.

"No doubt you'll realize you've lost the men in the house and throw yourself at my brother. He's rich enough for you though perhaps not as wealthy as Tomas, but Victor doesn't mind loud women in the same way as Tomas."

Victor choked on a cough and Violet turned toward her twin, smirking before facing the viper again. "You're welcome, dear. Maybe you can weasel your way into another wealthy bosom. You can try for my brother. But I'd really suggest you start fresh. Algernon is the kind to whine about being thrown over and telling tales, and Victor won't like that. Algie is a good one. You were stupid to give him up. A good man, with a good heart, easily led, easily wounded. Look at him now, daggers in his gaze."

Violet turned to Victor, who was unamused. "Oh look, Victor has already heard of your ways."

She tucked her arm through his and led him away. "Come now, brother dear. A little chasing is good for the wind. You know you need to run to stay fit. Get your blood racing. Bettina is a good huntress. She'll keep you in excellent order."

"The things I have done for you, and you just, just..."

"Save Tomas like that?"

Victor cleared his throat. "I should have known you'd claim to be helping him."

"Tomas asked me for mischief," Violet told her twin, laughing up into his face. "You should have been prepared."

Victor glanced at Violet. "I should have. I know you too well, sister devil."

There was another shriek from the stairs. Mr. Hull opened the door for the twins as they left the house, whispering as they passed him, "I am not sure that we shall survive, my lady."

"Of course you will," Violet said brightly. "Tell Beatrice to bring down one of my boxes of chocolates and some of Victor's liqueurs. Whatever else you think you might enjoy, we will gladly foot the bill for. Perhaps some sort of entertainment for the staff here."

Victor glanced at Violet and asked, with awe, "What have you done, pretty devil?"

She winked and said brightly, "They're tormenting the Boutets and Miss Marino for me. The hangers-on will be much less comfortable in the coming days. I don't expect the response to be positive."

Giles had brought the auto to the front of Tomas's house, and the twins left.

"Do you hear that?" Violet asked.

Victor glanced at her. "What's that now?"

"Nothing. There's nothing. No brash Italian voice. No furious shrieks. We must tip Tomas's servants very well when we leave."

Victor leaned back. "Beatrice gave me the new pages of the next book. I feel like you need to switch to a vampire story. Something with crypts and ghosts."

Violet sniffed. "I've titled it already. You can thank Bettina when she throws herself at you and presses her bosoms into your arm. It will be called, *Mr. Halicourt and the Scarlett Temptress*. What we're going to do is torment Isla and give her a happily ever after for this one."

Victor snorted and Violet patted his shoulder. "I've had more thought than that, brother dear. I am abound with ideas including what I think Tomas needs."

"What's that?"

"He needs Isolde," Violet said.

Victor choked, shaking his head in horror. "She's too young."

"Certainly. But she doesn't want to go to college. She's only saying she'll do it because it's what I want for her."

"Yes—" Victor coughed. "I have thought that for a while."

"You aren't the only matchmaker in this family, dear brother. Think about it. Tomas needs someone who anchors him, he has good memories with Isolde as well, and he can create more. He needs someone who will link him to us since we're the only foundation he has left after losing his family to the war and the flu. Tomas needs us, we cannot abandon him, but I won't marry him despite all that."

"And Isolde?" Victor demanded.

"She wants to marry. She wants to be loved and protected and spoiled. Do you remember how many times she stopped to coo over a perambulator?"

Victor snorted, but he didn't argue. They drove through the town and into the countryside, finding a river alongside the road and pulled over. They walked while the day passed and then headed towards the train. The twins discussed Tomas and Isolde, the people at Tomas's house, how to free them of the hangers-on, and their story. Victor was easily persuaded to the Scarlett Temptress title since he was also easily amused by the ridiculous.

The train had arrived early when they expected it to be late, and Violet ran up to her friends Lila and Gwennie, sitting on their trunks.

"Darlings," Violet called. "Darlings!" She threw herself into their arms and listened to them squeal.

"You'll never guess," Lila cut in after remarking on Vi's dress.

"Guess what, dear one?"

"Who was on the train," Lila said with an arch look. She glanced to the side and Violet turned to follow her gaze.

Victor was standing with Denny, John Davies, and Jack Wakefield. The sight of that man made Vi's heart leap right into her throat. She was utterly unprepared for the sight of him. He was a tall man, huge really, built like a bear or an oak tree or something else equally solid. Dark hair, dark eyes that pierced and noticed far more than you'd expect from a British man with an upper-class demeanor.

"Why Mr. Wakefield," Violet said cheerily, "we keep meeting on trains."

He grinned at her and held out his hand. Violet placed her hand in his. The feel of those strong fingers closing about hers was far more momentous than the movement warranted, as if she'd suddenly come home and the world which had been askew righted itself. To her surprise, he didn't let go but pulled her a little closer and tucked her hand through the crook in his elbow.

"What an interesting coincidence," Violet said, glancing at her brother.

"My father lives here," Jack said with a grin, but she felt

his gaze move over her face with nearly as much weight as a touch.

"Jack agreed to come to Tomas party tomorrow night," Victor said. "Isn't this fun? Then we'll all go back to London. Violet, for one, has business. Denny has to play at business, so his father will keep up his allowance. Jack—well..." Victor cocked his head at Jack. "You probably have real business."

"Indeed," Jack said with a bit of a snort.

"Shall we get a coffee together before we separate?" Victor suggested. "That bakery has tables, divine raspberry tarts, and the most wonderful tea."

"I can't," Jack said. "My father's man is here to take me to the house. We have an appointment. I delayed only long enough to say hello when I realized you were coming."

"Hullo," Violet said cheerily, as though she weren't disappointed. Her heart was racing as she stared at him and she found her wits had fled.

"May I have a moment?"

Violet nodded and he tugged her after him. "I wonder if I might convince you to go for a drive with me the morning after the party. I won't be in Kent for long."

"A drive does sound lovely," Violet said merrily, trying to hide how she was overwhelmed by seeing him so unexpectedly. She glanced back at her brother, saw his twitching mouth, and knew for certain it wasn't just their friends he'd called in.

She was both terribly sorry she'd told Bettina of his inheritance and terribly happy since he'd kept this secret from her.

"You'll be coming back to London soon?"

At Violet's nod, he said, "I'll be glad to see you there. Do you have a date for your arrival?"

"I believe Victor told Tomas that we'd be staying for a few days. Our birthday is in about a fortnight, and we intend on throwing ourselves a party in London. I hope that you'll come."

"I'll be there," Jack said. "Did you enjoy Bruges?"

Violet paused before she admitted, "I enjoyed the canals. I enjoyed the chocolate. So much. Shopping was fun. Getting to know Isolde without her mother around was priceless, but I wanted to be home. I missed...things here."

"You were missed," he said calmly, but he squeezed her hand as he said it, and she felt a flash of hope. She realized in that moment that her fear that he'd meet someone else had not come to pass. He had traveled this way to see his father but was taking time to see them. She glanced around and had to be honest with herself—he had separated her out because he wasn't there to see them. When it came right down to it, it was her.

CHAPTER NINE

There was dinner to be had before the party with the guests who were staying with Tomas. The party itself wouldn't be a large thing since they were in the country. Then, as soon as it was done, Violet and Victor needed to get rid of Tomas's hangers-on.

Violet considered her dresses for a while. "Beatrice. The peacock dress."

Her eyes lightened and she bounced on her toes a little. "I'll have it ready."

At its essence, it was a simple sleeveless black dress, but the beading on it imitated peacock feathers in silver and green. The dress ended just about her mid-thighs, but the green fringe on the dress went past her knees. Her headband had been made to go with the dress, with matching beads.

Violet decided to go with heavy eye makeup and bright red lips. It wouldn't be all that bright in the rooms open to the party, and she knew her eyes were one of her best features. With a woman like Juliette Boutet in the mix, Violet wanted to be at her best for when Jack appeared. She finished her apparel with a silver choker and several matching silver and emerald bangles that went well with her dress.

"Oh, my lady," Beatrice declared, "you look like a fanciful dream."

There was time yet before Violet needed to appear for the dinner, so she asked, "Tell me how things are going with Miss Marino and the French duo."

Beatrice's gaze widened. "It's been an uproar. Miss Marino requested a tray in her room, and they didn't deliver it until she'd requested it three times, and then they sent it with a weak chamomile, stale biscuits, and only bread and butter. She...well...Mary was found weeping later."

Violet sighed. "Give Mary some chocolate and a fiver from me."

Beatrice grinned and nodded. "I did tell Mary you'd make it better. Thank you, my lady."

"Anything else?"

Beatrice nodded. "The Boutets have not made a complaint at all. But there has been quite a ruckus in Miss Boutet's room between them. I asked, but no one heard what it is about."

"What about Mr. Stroud or Algie?"

"Mr. Algernon left during the afternoon. His man said he went to the hotel to talk to Mr. Theodophilus." Violet shuddered and Beatrice echoed it. She had refused to leave Violet when Theo had assaulted her, securing Vi's unending loyalty.

"Mr. Stroud was seen leaving Miss Marino's bedroom very early this morning."

Vi's brows rose and she stood. It was past time to meet the others for cocktails before dinner. They'd eat and then the rest of the guests would arrive. Violet walked down to her brother's room, knocking on the door.

"Hullo, luvie," he said. "You look simply smashing."

Violet grinned at him. "You as well, darling. I rather like that suit."

"Must be because you pressured me to buy it," he said with a wink.

"I was so right too!"

They walked down the stairs and paused in shock to see that Mr. Stroud had Juliette Boutet in his arms. She struggled to free herself. That was bad enough, but just out of sight of the couple was François Boutet, watching his sister try and fail to free herself.

Violet's gaze narrowed and she faked a sneeze. Mr. Stroud looked up as the twins walked down the stairs. He let go of Juliette, who backed away, breathing heavily.

Violet wound her arm through Juliette's. "Don't you look just lovely." The twins pulled Juliette towards the dining room and Violet asked, "Did you need a moment?" She knew she could use one.

Juliette smiled with a shaky lip and shook her head. Violet nodded, determined to put on the same, brave front. When they entered the room where everyone else was waiting, Victor approached Tomas. "These ladies need a drink."

Tomas started and looked at the twins with clouded eyes that didn't quite see them. Violet and Victor glanced at each other. Things weren't looking positive.

Violet put Juliette's drink in her trembling hand and kept near her until their mutual shaking had ceased. Once Juliette seemed gathered, Violet excused herself to join her brother. Victor handed her a second drink with a murmur. "There may not be enough cocktails to navigate these fraught waters. Do you feel as though everyone is wearing a mask?"

Violet glanced at her brother, noted his clenching jaw, and placed her hand on his arm.

"Yes, all of them. Even Tomas, that fiendish brother, poor Juliette."

"Is Miss Boutet all right?" Victor asked softly.

Violet shook her head. Too many women wore that mask. She took a sip of her cocktail. "Is that the orange liqueur?"

The question wasn't because she cared but because she needed to think of something else. "I so look forward to our own house."

"As do I," Victor said grimly, but he wouldn't let the matter drop. "She might be all right, but her brother is in danger of a severe beating."

Violet glanced towards François Boutet. She had to put on her own mask as she looked him over. He was tall, slim, and his eyes were darting between his sister and Mr. Stroud with the occasional frown towards Bettina Marino. Mr. Boutet's gaze fixed on his sister with rage.

Was he upset that his sister hadn't succumbed to Mr. Stroud or was he upset that she had been caught by Stroud?

The butler was maneuvering through the guests and Violet crossed to him. "How are things, Mr. Hull?"

He had a tight expression about his eyes. "My lady..."

"Oh, Mr. Hull, be brave," she told him. "Better to torment her now and get rid of her than have her win the war and be saddled with her."

He shuddered at that.

"Moments like these are why you are priceless," she told him, "and why Mr. St. Marks counts on you so. You and the rest of the staff."

The dinner was awkward. Tomas was jumpy, and Violet guessed something had happened to trigger his ghosts. He seemed as though he were entirely unaware of what was happening.

It didn't help that Bettina was furious and so loud, Violet wished to shove a handkerchief into the woman's mouth. Violet cleared her throat and stared at her brother until he glanced her way. Her gaze moved to Bettina, and then Vi raised her brow at Victor.

He knew what she wanted, winced, and drained his glass before he turned a charming smile on Bettina.

"Tomas," Violet asked softly. She was seated at his right,

and she took his wine glass, draining it. She shook her head at Mr. Hull when he stepped forward to refill it. She raised a brow, and he nodded. Only a minute later he placed a new glass in front of Tomas, filled with water.

He didn't even seem to notice the switch as he drained it.

"Do you remember," Violet asked lightly, "that time when we were children and we decided that we needed to pool our funds and buy as many raspberry tarts as possible from the bakery?"

Tomas blinked in her direction, not seeing her, and she kept talking with her hand on his wrist. She described the taste of the tarts, the way the sun had shone down on them, running through the woods near the stream to swim after eating them. As she spoke, Tomas stared in her direction, slowly coming back to himself.

He stared around the dining room as if surprised to find them there. "Vi..."

"Tomas," she replied merrily, squeezing his wrist.

"I...this...I'm sorry."

"Tomas," Violet repeated, so low that only he could hear her. "I will jabber at you as often as you need."

He shuddered and whispered back, "My house is at war. I feel like I've been invaded by shrieking geese."

"A war we'll win," she said cheerily and then added a little louder, "Tomas, I need your assistance with some business matters. Do you think that you could travel back to London when Victor and I go?"

"Yes," Victor said, having caught enough of the invitation to talk around Bettina. "I also have some ideas about things that I need your advice on."

"Enough business," Bettina declared, her gaze narrowing. "I'm sure we'd all be happy to go with you to London."

Victor smiled down at her, but the lion was in his gaze as he asked, "Oh, were you thinking of coming to London as well?"

She fluttered her lashes at him. "We can't have our friendship come to such a swift end."

Victor cocked his head. "Well, perhaps we'll run into each other there."

Bettina's gaze narrowed and she turned to Tomas, but Victor drew her attention back to him. Her anger hadn't faded, but she was trying to hide it behind her allure.

"Tomas," Violet said idly, "how do you feel about Monaco?"

"I don't know that I have thoughts about Monaco," he said.

"You should think on it," Violet said. "I have need of your assistance in Monaco as well."

Violet was dancing with Tomas when Jack arrived. When the song came to an end, they headed to the side of the room and Jack appeared through the cigarette smoke clouding the air.

"Hullo," Tomas said, staring in confusion at Jack as if wondering whether they knew each other. Maybe they did? Perhaps he recognized Jack and didn't realize why. Perhaps Tomas wasn't quite certain what was happening around him and was confused by the people in his house.

"Tomas, my friend, this is Jack Wakefield. Jack, Tomas St. Marks."

Tomas's jaw clenched and when they shook hands, Tomas attempted to crush Jack's hand while pretending to smile. Violet sighed and Tomas glanced at her. There was a crashing sound from the band and Tomas leapt in his skin, a look of horror crossing his face. He blinked stupidly down at Violet, then said shakily, "Hot in here, inn't? I think I'll get some air."

There was another crash from the band, the trumpeter tripping over something and landing against the fellow with a bass. Tomas rushed out of the room. She looked after him, worried, and glanced around for Victor, but if he were there, she couldn't find him.

Jack examined Violet's face, followed her gaze after Tomas, and with a clenched jaw, Jack asked Violet to dance as the band got themselves put back together.

The feel of his hands against her back, on her waist, jerked her attention from Tomas, and Vi grinned up at Jack as the music started. They danced through song after song until Violet declared, "I must have a drink."

Tomas had placed a cart for making drinks in the room along with having servants circulating with trays of cocktails. The cart was for Victor, but Violet and Jack made use of it. Violet popped a piece of ice into her mouth while Jack created them a cocktail.

"So, Tomas," Jack said as he shook the cocktail shaker that he'd filled with cognac, orange liqueur, and lemon juice. Violet put ice in the cups for them and he filled their drinks. "He is the man who offered for you? The reason you could say you didn't kill your aunt?"

Violet knew that Jack remembered. She was wondering why he said it with such bite. Was it because she was here with Tomas? She could understand that. She had to admit that she wouldn't have been delighted to discover him at the home of a woman who had been chasing him.

The anger in his voice, however, triggered a corresponding fury in Violet that caused her to say sharply, "I didn't kill my aunt." It wasn't so much her words as her anger that had Jack glancing at her.

He searched her face. "Yes, I know. Of course."

"So, Tomas's offer or lack thereof..."

"I—" Jack started, but yet again, one of Bettina's shrieks interrupted.

They turned and saw Juliette and Bettina struggling together. Her hands were clawed and aimed towards the dancer's face with Juliette holding Bettina back by her wrists.

A broken cocktail glass was at their feet, the glass and drink sprayed around their feet. With the second shriek, the band came to a screeching stop as the guests turned to stare at the commotion.

The audience only seemed to enliven Bettina, who screamed, "Whore!"

Juliette replied, but she spoke too low for Violet to hear.

Bettina's reply was another furious, "Whore! Thief!"

Even though Juliette was smaller than Bettina, Juliette didn't have any trouble holding the Italian off. Bettina was all curves whereas Juliette was an athlete. A moment later, it came to an end when Charles Stroud hooked his arm around Bettina's waist and hauled her off. He chuckled, seemingly delighted by the fight. Bettina in hand, he nodded to the band and pulled her from the room.

The music started again with a screech.

"What kind of people are you spending your time with?" Jack asked Violet.

Violet glanced at him, saw disgust in his face, and had to bite back a furious response. She wasn't going to defend Tomas to Jack. Or Tomas's companions. Not because Tomas didn't deserve it, but because she didn't deserve it. She didn't have to explain anything.

She grabbed her cocktail.

"Vi..." Jack started, taking hold of her bicep, but she twisted away.

She tossed her cocktail back and said, "Oh, look, Lila. How I've missed *her*."

Violet walked away from him and towards Lila and Denny, who were standing near a window watching the dancing. John and Gwennie were on the dance floor, but Violet just needed to move before she lashed out at Jack and regretted it later. She was already regretting being stupid enough to put Jack and Tomas in the same room. Especially with Tomas as fragile as he was.

"Uh oh," Lila said when she took in Violet's expression. "These people of Tomas are quite...interesting aren't they? I find myself fascinated by them and cannot wait to see what they'll do next. The fact that they've left the room makes me quite want to wander the halls for the next episode."

Violet smiled at her friends, laughing at Lila, but it was a pure lie and they all knew it.

"Jack," Lila whispered a moment later to warn Violet that he was approaching. "Isn't the music lovely?" she said aloud. "I do love a good trumpet player."

Violet winded her arms through Lila's. She glanced at Jack. Behind him, she took in an entirely unexpected sight and screamed as though the hounds of hell were coming for her.

Jack responded without thinking. He grabbed Violet, yanking her from Lila and shoving her behind his back as he turned to face the threat.

Violet wormed away, darting around Jack and ignoring his shout as she threw herself at the man who'd stumbled into the room, startling her so. "Tomas?"

"Violet!" Jack shouted.

Tomas clutched her like a drowning man. He dropped to his knees, wrapped his arms around her waist, and pressed his face into her stomach. His trembling was terrifying, and Violet was well aware that he was stuck in his memories, fighting ghosts that only he could see.

The music had stopped at Violet's scream, and the dancers stared in horror at Violet being held by the blood-covered Tomas. The whispers started, the low questions to each other. "Is that blood? Is that Tomas? Who is that girl? Are they together? Whose blood is that?"

Violet ignored all of the questions and placed her hand in Tomas's hair. "Tomas?"

He shuddered in reply, finally asking, "Vi?" He asked like a scared child. "Vi, is that really you? I used to imagine you when I was so cold in the trenches. When...oh God, Vi.

There was so much blood. There's always so much blood. So much I could taste it. Pieces of my friends on my skin. Oh God, Vi..." He looked up her. "Am I really home? Is this real?"

Violet ignored everyone and dropped to her knees in front of Tomas, her skin crawling at the blood she could feel, the smell of it, the...was she tasting it too?

She cupped his face between her two palms. "Tomas, this is real. You are home. This is your house. Mrs. Newstone will have Cook make jam tarts, and we'll eat them until we're sick."

A tear rolled down his cheek. "Do you promise?"

She nodded. "I promise, my friend. I promise. You're home. The war is over."

"But I'm so cold."

She didn't know what to say to that. She glanced at Jack and hissed to him. "Get these people out of here."

Lila acted even when Jack didn't.

"Out," Lila snapped. "Out this way. Come on now."

Violet gave Tomas her full attention. "We should think about swimming again. Remember when we'd jump in and see who could dunk the others the most? Remember the way the water felt against your skin? The sun overhead? The way we'd swim until our muscles ached and then we'd lay in the sun to dry? Only to go home and get in so much for trouble for looking like gypsy children? Silly adults, we looked like children who'd played the day away."

"Violet," Jack interrupted. "He's bloody!"

"I know," Violet hissed. "I know."

She didn't even know what she was saying after that, only that she talked and Tomas slowly came back to himself.

"Blood, Vi, so much blood."

"Whose is it?"

"It's...it's...it's...Bettina. It's Bettina."

"Bettina? Where?"

"The folly, Vi. Bloody hell, Vi. She was still alive. I tried. I tried to help. Just like with Tommy. With Chuck. With Ben. He was so young. The little blighter had to have lied to join up. I can still see their faces. I can see them every time I close my eyes. Why was Bettina bloody? The war is over. It's over. You promised. You said I was all done."

Tomas was crying and Violet cried with him. She looked up at Jack, tears rolling down her face as Tomas rocked back and forth, arms still clutched around her waist.

"Victor can show you where," Violet told Jack.

"Victor isn't here," Jack said. "We have to find her. If she was alive..."

"I can help," Denny said. "I know where the folly is."

Jack started snapping orders to the servants finishing with, "Get the police here."

CHAPTER TEN

Violet sang to Tomas until Mr. Hull and Victor arrived. Lullabies, humming without words, until her voice was hoarse fighting back the sound of weeping to give Tomas the comfort of a song instead.

"He won't get better until the blood is gone, my lady. Let me take him."

Violet nodded and Mr. Hull lifted Tomas up like a baby to carry him out of the empty party room. Violet watched them go until Victor squatted down by her. "Vi? Darling?"

She slowly turned to him and gasped, "Look at all this blood. How did he stand it? Over and over again? Friend after friend?"

"Darling, he didn't stand it. That's why he is like he is." Victor pulled on Violet until she stood and then he lifted her into his arms.

"Let's get that off of you, shall we? You'll feel so much better when it's gone."

"I think I can taste it too."

"Then you'll need to brush your teeth first," Victor said

grimly. He tried and failed for a cheery tone. "Though I'm certain there is no blood in your mouth, sweet sister."

Victor carried Violet to her bedroom through a side door, avoiding where the party goers had been taken. The hall on the other side of the door was empty but for the housekeeper.

Victor almost groaned with relief when he saw Mrs. Newstone. "Beatrice, immediately. Then both brandy and tea. Right now, please."

"Of course, Mr. Victor."

Victor hurried to Violet's room and set her down on a chair. He walked into her bath to turn the water on. When he came back into her bedroom, Beatrice had arrived.

Violet knew she was shaking, that her mind wasn't working quite right. The reality of being covered in Bettina's blood had sent her mind for a spiral where she couldn't quite grasp the nature of her thoughts.

Beatrice took one look at Vi. "Oh, no."

"She'll be all right," Victor said. "She just needs the blood off."

Vi rose. "I just need...." She shook her head and walked into the bath. She had blood on her hands. She scrubbed at them until the water ran clean and then took the toothbrush that Victor handed her. Beatrice pulled on Violet here and there until Violet realized that her jewelry had been removed. Violet brushed her teeth until Victor took her toothbrush away.

At some point, Tomas must have grabbed her hair, and she could feel it hardening with blood. Violet yanked off her headband, kicked off her shoes, and stared helplessly at the bath. She shut the door to block Victor, stripped off her dress, and dropped into the water.

Victor had done a terrible job filling the bath and the water was cold. Little matter. Violet slathered her body with soap once, rinsed, washed again, rinsed, and then she let the water out of the tub. Kneeling in the draining water, she washed her body again.

"My lady?" Beatrice asked. "My lady. Do you need anything?"

Violet started the water, rinsing out the tub, and then filling it again. "Brandy, please."

"She must be doing better," Victor said from the bedroom, "if she's ready for a drink."

Her twin sounded as though he were grasping at straws, and he *was* because she was very much *not* doing better.

Violet lay back in the bath, adding bubbles to the water. She'd already washed her hair twice, but she started for a third time with the hottest water she could stand. She would have lingered in the water, but Victor needed to think she was all right before he could go track down whether or not Bettina had survived and just what was happening. Violet washed her body again, rinsed again, and rose, drying quickly before donning her robe.

She rubbed a towel over her hair and walked back into her bedroom. "I'm fine, Victor. Go see what is happening."

Victor had changed while she bathed. He examined her face. "If I go...you will lock this door for anyone but me and Jack."

"Of course, Mr. Victor," Beatrice said. "Of course."

"Take care of my sister, Beatrice," Victor said. "Just take care."

Violet dressed into pajamas and her kimono as soon as Victor was gone. She hadn't noticed it at the time, but she saw that Beatrice had cleaned Violet's jewelry and removed the gown.

"It's happened again, I think," Violet told Beatrice. "I'll have to give you a raise, my dear. Taking care of me when our lives keep running into bodies and crimes."

"You already pay me better than most maids, my lady," Beatrice said. "Working for you is the best thing that happened to me. I love it. You travel, you have beautiful clothes to take care of, you are kind and generous."

A tear slipped down her face and Beatrice begged, "Please don't cry, my lady."

There was a knock at the door, and Violet and Beatrice turned to it. Both of them calculated who was on the other side. What danger they faced. Bettina had been hurt. If it was a malicious attack, were they in danger as well?

"It's me, Vi," Lila called. "Gwennie and I and a tea tray. We've been instructed by the boys to bolt ourselves in."

Violet nodded and Beatrice slowly opened the door. Her friends were on the other side with Mrs. Newstone. Beatrice let them in and then locked the bedroom door again.

Violet took the seat at her desk as the others found places around the room. "Come in and join us, Mrs. Newstone, Beatrice. This isn't a time to stand on whatever nonsense keeps us from sitting down together with a good cup of tea and better gossip."

"Mr. Hull asked me to check on you when I went to see how Mr. Tomas was doing."

"Is Tomas all right?" Violet asked.

Mrs. Newstone considered and then shook her head. "No, my dear. I'm afraid he is very much not all right."

"Bloody hell," Lila muttered, "why couldn't we just have a party? What happened? Who is this person who has been injured?"

"Do we know what happened to her?" Violet had washed rather a disturbing amount of blood from her body. Just how much could Bettina lose and still be alive? By Jove, she must be dead. She must be. Vi couldn't imagine otherwise, but what did she know of what humans could survive? Very little, as spoiled as she'd been since the day of her birth.

Mrs. Newstone shook her head. "Some of the staff might have heard. I'll find out."

Beatrice opened the bedroom door for Mrs. Newstone, let her out, and locked it again.

"She must be dead," Violet said.

"Who is this woman? Bettina? Is that right?" Lila glanced at Gwennie, who was pale. "Darling, you'll be fine," Lila reassured her. "You were with John. We'll have him take you home as soon as can be."

"Bettina Marino," Violet said, answering Lila's question.

"Why would anyone want to hurt her?"

Beatrice choked and Violet glanced her way. The two of them who had met and dealt with Bettina considered each other.

"It really is a matter of who wouldn't want to hurt her," Violet said. "She is an awful woman."

Lila gasped and Vi explained what she'd witnessed of Bettina, finishing with, "To be honest, I think that she was playing the men against each other. Making them vie for her as though she were some prize instead of a fortune hunter. She was furious when she thought I had stolen Tomas from her and when Victor was uninterested."

"She sounds awful," Lila said. "You always do find the most interesting people."

"Like you, for instance?" Violet asked.

"I would say so, though to be fair, Gwennie is utterly normal. She even wants babies as soon as she can persuade John to put a ring on her finger."

Violet shot Gwennie a look and shook her head. "Foolish girl," Violet murmured. "He should be persuading you to *allow* him to put a ring on your finger."

Lila laughed with delight and crowed, "Hear, hear!"

Gwennie shook her head. "I'm not anything special. The fact that John—"

Lila and Violet groaned while Gwennie glanced between them.

"What?" Gwennie understood nothing.

There was another knock on the door and Mrs. Newstone called into the room. Her tone was answer enough, but they opened the door. A sensible grey dress, comfortable shoes, hair pulled back into a knot at the base of her neck, white face with brilliant red circles on her cheekbones.

"She's...she's...Miss Marino is..."

"She's dead," Violet said for the housekeeper.

Mrs. Newstone helplessly shook her head. "Murdered." She choked a little as though the word were a knot in her throat, but she wasn't finished. "Murdered at the folly and my master is the suspect."

CHAPTER ELEVEN

There were times when one had to disregard promises. Violet slowly stood. She had dressed in pajamas after her bath, so she flung open her armoire doors, found the first dress, and put it on while Lila and Gwennie demanded what she was up to.

Violet didn't reply, she just dressed and left her room. Tomas's bedroom was in the other wing, but Violet knew the house well enough to make her way there without anyone but servants seeing her. When she reached the door, she heard Jack and Victor shouting at each other. Violet pushed the door open and both of them turned to her.

"Get out," Violet said. "Get out right now."

"He needs to be questioned," Jack argued.

"Violet," Victor said, but she shot him a look that said he was as much a part of the problem. Victor's gaze narrowed on Violet, but she ignored him and faced Jack.

"Yes," Violet agreed, "he needs to be questioned. But you fought in the war, Jack. I'm sure you've seen this before. Tomas isn't going to be able to answer questions if you don't let me calm him down. Once he does calm down, he'll respond to my questions."

"Violet, if you think I'm going to leave you here with this man who probably killed that poor woman, you are mad." Jack's shout startled her, as did the way he grabbed her arm.

She screamed a little and then reminded herself that it was Jack who would never hurt her.

"Let go of my sister," Victor warned.

"Vic! Stop it! You need to leave," she said precisely. "You both need to leave right now."

"There is no part of me that is playing games with your safety, Violet," Jack told her.

She searched his face and knew that he would not negotiate with her on this. Slowly, Violet cleared her throat. She glanced at Victor, who shook his head at her. He wasn't leaving either.

With a sigh, Violet said, "Stand back and be quiet."

"Tomas wouldn't hurt Bettina, Vi," her twin said. He didn't sound convinced and Violet's furious glare had her brother crossing his arms over his chest.

"*You* know better than to be shouting like this, Victor."

"We'll both quiet down," Jack said, taking Victor's arm and pulling him to stand next to the wall. Violet searched both of their faces. They were both angry, and that anger extended to Violet, which infuriated her as well.

She turned on her heel before she started shouting, too, and crossed to where Mr. Hull was physically keeping Tomas in the armchair near the fire. Tomas's hands were over his ears, and his panic made her even angrier.

"Thank you, my lady," Mr. Hull whispered. "I wish you would be our mistress. Mr. Tomas needs you, ma'am."

Violet ignored the butler and pulled the second chair closer so she could take Tomas's hand.

"Tomas," Violet said gently. "Tomas." Violet waited, saying his name again and again until he looked her way. She sighed as his lost eyes met hers. "When Aunt Agatha met you for the first time, she said you were a grubby little boy who was clearly going to spend his days ensconced in mischief and hijinks."

Tomas looked dully up at Violet, not really seeing her.

"I'm going to tell you a secret," Violet told him cheerily, as though she weren't dying inside. As though Jack and Victor's anger weren't making her want to flee them all. "Aunt Agatha told me later, after you left, to make sure I got into as much mischief with you as I could. She said you had a good heart. She said that mischief with someone who had a good heart was the way to live your life."

Tomas seemed to latch onto that. "You don't want me."

Violet smiled and kissed his forehead. "For mischief? Always."

There was a shuffling from near the wall, but Violet didn't turn that way. She kept her gaze and her hand on Tomas, keeping him anchored to her.

"You told me you were going to make Bettina miserable," Tomas said. "Our last mischief was to make her miserable. Vi...she died in my arms. She...she was so scared. She begged me to help her."

Violet bit her lip. By Jove, she thought, they had. "We weren't going to hurt her. Just make her want to move on to another rich fellow. It wasn't our fault she died, it was our fault she got cold tea and stale bread with her tea. Mischief, my friend, not murder."

"Vi, I..."

Violet glanced at Jack, who had his hands on his hips, staring at them. He was furious. So angry, she could feel it crackling. She swallowed on a dry throat. She had no idea those penetrating eyes could be so very harsh.

"Tell me what happened," she urged Tomas, giving him her full attention once more.

Tomas stared into the fire. "The ghosts have been

haunting me for weeks, Vi. For weeks and weeks. I don't know what made it start, but I thought..."

"It's why you came to Bruges?"

"I thought you and Victor could help me. The last time it was so bad."

"I understand," she said softly. "I know why you came to Bruges. Tell me about tonight. What about when the trumpet player tripped? You left because of the noise. You went to walk it off."

Tomas was shaking as Violet squeezed his hand, and he grasped hers, his fingers digging in too hard, but she hid the pain to keep him talking.

"They were already there in the shadows," he whispered. "The ghosts. I keep seeing Ben. It's always Ben. Everyone else changes, but Ben...God, Vi, he was so young. He was so earnest. Such a good kid. He was the type who would do whatever it took to make things better. He used to tell jokes. Who tells jokes in the trenches, Vi?"

Violet shook her head. It was a question no one would answer, could answer. "Then what happened? Tonight?"

"The band...it was so loud. It was like they were shooting again. Like in the trenches. It all came back, so I did what we talked about. I went for a walk, I focused on the swimming holes, and on the tarts. That day at the fair."

"You did just right," Violet said, gently. She had to whisper because Tomas was squeezing far too hard, and it was difficult to hide the pain of it. "You did just right. What happened next?"

She glanced over to Jack and Victor, who were staring furiously at each other. Jack waved his hand, and she scowled at both of them.

"Tomas," Violet said gently, "what happened next?"

"I...I...don't know. I...walked for so long. I walked until I was freezing. I was so cold. I'm always cold, Vi. Always."

"I know, Tomas," Violet said. "I know. When did you get to the folly?"

"I don't know. I don't know. I don't know."

"Tomas!"

He slowly turned up to her face and blinked at her.

"Was she there when you arrived? How did you find her?"

"I..." His head tilted as he considered. "She must have been there already. There wasn't anyone. I paced it. Like I used to. I paced it, and I went past the tower. I was by that pile of rocks. The one you said was so dumb when we were little."

Violet nodded.

"That's when I saw her. She was lying there in the blood. She was whimpering with it. She gasped. That rattling gasp, I've heard it so many times. I knew she was going to die, but I tried. I pulled out the knife, I used my coat to put pressure on the wound, I held her. It's so hard to die alone. I held her tightly and I lied. I told her it would be okay."

He was crying, and Violet cried with him. Her voice was shaking and the gasps of pain from his grip were disguised by the tears she shed with Tomas. "Was anyone else there?"

He shook his head. "I wasn't seeing right, Vi. I was seeing Ben. Always Ben. I didn't see her, not really. I was talking to him, not to her."

"I know, my friend. I know. Tell us the rest."

"She was still alive. She was crying. She was cold too. She always seemed so fiery. She shouldn't have been cold. Hell isn't hot, Vi. It's cold. It's cold and wet and when she died, I should have been talking to her, not to him."

Violet nodded. Tomas turned to the fire and she could see the ghosts were reaching for him.

"Mr. Hull," she said quietly, "don't let him drink. Have his man stay with him. Don't leave him alone. Someone read to him."

Mr. Hull nodded, and Vi added, "He always liked *Alice in Wonderland* when we were little. Nothing suspenseful."

Mr. Hull nodded and Violet twisted her wrist away from Tomas, biting back a gasp. He didn't seem to notice, his hands moving to grip the arms of his chair instead.

Violet put her hand behind her back so Jack and Victor wouldn't see the forming bruises. She pointed at the door with her uninjured hand and waited until Jack and Victor stepped out of the room first.

"Let's argue in the library," she said, "before we push Tomas further into his memories."

Victor swept his hand in front of him, and Violet led the way. When they reached the library, they all turned on each other.

"He thinks Tomas killed that woman," Victor said, furious. "He won't listen to me."

"Of course he does," Violet said, putting one hand against her forehead. It was pounding and her wrist ached.

"So you're on his side? Because you're infatuated?" Victor demanded. "You're going to throw over Tomas for him?"

"I'm on his side because I can use my brain," Violet shot back. "You should try it. Jack doesn't know Tomas. Tomas is a dangerous man—"

"Dangerous?" Victor shouted. "What is wrong with you? He's our friend."

"He was a soldier," Jack answered for Violet. "It comes with the territory."

Violet took in a deep breath and let it out slowly. "Stop yelling, Victor, or my inner shrew will torture you for ages."

Victor shot her a nasty look. "What is wrong with you, Violet? Why are you being like this?"

"I was covered in Bettina's blood," Violet told him softly. "I would be curled up in my bed, crying about it, but Tomas needs us."

"And yet you're defending Jack, who has already decided that Tomas did it!"

"Tomas *was* in the army for a couple of years," Violet told Victor. "He's not the same as he was before the war. I know you feel guilty. I know your arm was broken and you didn't end up in the trenches, and then the war was over. I know that makes you feel guilty. You feel like you should have at least suffered alongside and lived or died with them."

"Vi, why are you saying these things?" Victor demanded.

"Because you feel guilty that you aren't haunted like Tomas is. It's not your fault that your friends died or are damaged and you aren't."

Victor punched the wall.

Violet turned to Jack, undeterred. "They are closer than brothers, Jack. And Victor feels responsible for Tomas."

"So he's giving you to Tomas?"

"I am not chattel," Violet snapped, "or something to be given."

"Vi!" Victor said. "Tomas needs us..."

"Listen," Violet told Jack softly, "you're right. Tomas is dangerous, but his inherent nature is gentle and kind. I understand why you suspect Tomas. It seems logical, but you're wrong."

Jack growled a little as he said, "Violet, he was covered in her blood."

"Yes, I know."

"He was lost in his memories. He said that himself. It's possible he didn't know what he was doing, but that doesn't mean he is innocent."

"You don't know him like Victor and I do," Violet snapped. Her head hurt, her wrist hurt, her heart hurt.

"There have been soldiers who have killed their wives while stuck in memories of the past. The people they love the most, Violet. Your Tomas isn't infallible. You don't know what he did. You were with me. You're the only one who I am certain didn't hurt Bettina."

Violet took in a slow breath and let it out before she spoke. "Bettina was a fortune hunter who wound up the men around her and played them off of each other. She targeted every man in the house, some who were actually bothered by her antics because she insulted their pride and their manhood. Tomas was not one of them. There are other people who had motives to kill her, Jack. You can't just disregard that."

Jack looked up at the ceiling. "Throwing other people out as suspects doesn't change the fact that we found him covered in her blood. There are policemen out there fingerprinting the knife that killed her, and it will have his prints on it, Violet. There's nothing I can do."

"You could trust us," Violet suggested. "You could trust that Victor and I have been witnesses of Tomas in all of his memories. Do you know what he does? He curls up into a ball and rocks back and forth with his hands over his ears. He cries and talks to dead men. You could recognize that we have reasons for why we're so sure. Years of them."

"You don't need a motive if you're shell-shocked, Vi," Jack said gently.

"Is it so hard to accept that we might be right?"

"He's jealous, Vi," Victor said. "Denny told me about how Tomas clutched you like a life raft. Any man would be jealous after that."

Violet's gaze darted to Jack, whose face was expressionless. She pressed her uninjured hand over her mouth. "Bettina had relations with Mr. Stroud, Algie, possibly François Boutet, and she was overtly pursuing Tomas and Victor. What if you were a less principled man, Jack? What would you do? All we're asking is that you trust us to know our childhood friend well. I swear to you, Tomas did *not* do this."

"What do you want from me?" Jack demanded.

"I want you to investigate with the assumption that Victor and I could be right."

"Do you love him?"

"Yes," Violet said.

Jack's jaw clenched, she could see the muscle clenching in his jaw.

"She's always loved him, you fool," Victor said. "We both have. He's like a brother to both of us. That's all."

Jack didn't believe. Violet could see it in his face. She could see it in the way he stared at her hips and it took her a moment to realize Jack was fixated on where Tomas had clutched at her. They were fools. All of them.

"Fine," Jack said. "Fine."

He slammed from the room, leaving the twins staring at each other.

"You yelled at me," Violet told Victor. "You acted like I wasn't on your side or Tomas's side."

He rubbed his hands through his hair and slammed out of the library, only to come back in and state, "We don't know who killed Bettina. I won't leave you alone. This house isn't safe anymore."

She smacked his arm, pushed past him, and ran up the stairs. Victor followed after until Violet reached her room. She slammed the door in his face and then opened it, smacked his arm again and then slammed it in his face.

"Lock the door," Victor shouted.

Violet shrieked in reply.

"Oh my," Lila said. "I didn't think you two fought."

"Out," Violet declared. "Just out, please."

"Vi..." Gwennie started.

Lila cut in, "Gwen, love. When the twins fight, lesser mortals flee. Come now, darling."

CHAPTER TWELVE

Violet paced. There was no sleeping while she was as alienated as she was. Things might be—probably were—ruined with Jack. Victor was angry with her, making her feel like she was drowning. Tomas was lost to the memories. She frowned. What had she said when they were arguing? She wasn't chattel. She was the one who decided what she wanted, and she'd be making her own choices.

Aunt Agatha had raised Violet to be more proactive than pacing in her bedroom, bemoaning that she'd made the men in her life upset. Enough was enough. Violet wasn't going to wait for Jack. Or for Victor. This needed to end.

Violet had business to conduct. She had a life beyond the murder of that fiend of a woman who did not deserve to die but definitely deserved a good, hard slap. First the murder. Then Helen Mather's baby. Then Violet would decide what happened next.

Violet considered her options. It was late, but there was one person she could start with: easily-led Algernon. She walked to Algernon's bedroom and knocked on the door.

As she did, Jack came up the stairs. He had his notebook

in his hand and he eyed her with a furious frown. "What are you doing?"

"Talking to my cousin." She didn't smile. His gaze searched hers, and she wasn't sure what he saw, but he wasn't pleased.

"Talking to your cousin or looking for information?"

She smiled at him. "Did you find out who was actually in the room when Bettina died? Were the policemen able to remove people as suspects?"

"I see," he said, ignoring her question. "You are going to question your cousin, who may well have killed this woman. Do you think he won't hurt you if he killed her?"

Violet shrugged and saw Jack's jaw tick. She was getting a whole new skill set at making him angry. "Did you want to come in as well?"

"You need to go back to your room." His voice was a snap of fury.

"Yes, of course," Violet said, opening the door to Algernon's room and going inside.

"Violet," Jack called.

She ignored him and sat herself down in one of the chairs by Algernon's fireplace. She had turned on the light when she entered his room, but he wore an eye mask and didn't move in his bed.

Could he really be asleep or was he just pretending? She had no desire to shake him awake, so she grabbed the nearest book and threw it towards him. It smacked into his back and he grunted.

"Algie," Violet said, "sit up or I'll throw something else."

He snuffled rather like a pig. "What the devil?"

"Algie," Violet snapped.

He pushed off his eye mask and stared at her. She could tell by his bleary gaze he had been sleeping. How did he slip off into sleep's embrace without a care in the world?

"Violet, why are you here?" He was wearing pajamas, in his

bed. She was, she knew, being completely inappropriate by entering his room. Jack was there, Algie was her cousin, and there was a murderer afoot. "What is going on? Is that you, Jack?"

"It's me," Jack said, glancing at Violet and lifting his brow.

"What the devil?" Algie asked again, pulling his covers up to tuck them into his armpits. "Go away."

"No," Violet said. "Where were you? You weren't at the party when Tomas came in."

"Why do you say that?"

"Because you scream like a girl, and you would have screamed when Tomas showed up bloody."

"I do not," Algie said with a squeak. "I would not have."

"Where were you?"

Algie glanced away, a sure sign he didn't want to say, and Violet's gaze lowered on him. If they had been ten years old, she'd have been able to say with surety that it was Algie who'd stolen the tarts. Algie set his jaw and refused to answer.

Violet sighed. He'd used the same tactic as children. "Bettina is dead, Algie. You were...associated...with her. When you add in that Tomas is family and he's the main suspect here, you will answer."

"Tomas?" Algie demanded. He glanced at Jack and laughed nervously before shaking his head. "No, I can't believe that. Remember when we found that dog? It was vicious, and Tomas took care of it even though it bit him a good number of times."

"The war changes people," Jack told Algie. "The memories make him dangerous."

"I...don't know about that. Not Tomas."

"Where were you?" Violet demanded. "Answer the question, you fool."

"Well, ah...I had an appointment to...ah..."

"What?" Jack demanded. "Out with it, man."

"I had an appointment to see Theo. I rather owed him

some money. Went to find him around the time Jack came in. Why are you asking me? I heard about that catfight between Juliette and Bettina. Maybe it had a second round, eh? Got a bit out of hand? Makes more sense to me than *Tomas*. Ladies aren't rational creatures. You know that, Jack."

Violet did throw the next thing she laid her hands on, an ashtray, at Algie. A catfight? Not rational? Coming from this fool?

Violet growled under her breath. "And did you find Theo?"

"No...ah...I wasn't able to find him. So...well...by the time I got back inside, the party had been moved and everyone was being sorted by the bobbies, and well...I just nipped up the stairs to my room instead. More comfortable, you know. Long day. Big dinner. A good sleep seemed like just the thing."

"When we were children, you used to get all choppy with your answers. It was always how Aunt Agatha knew you were hiding something."

"I'm not hiding anything!" Algie squeaked.

"Mmmm," Violet said with sheer mockery that made Algie flush a brilliant red.

"No call to be cruel. I liked Bettina. Wouldn't have killed her. She was a fiery thing. And by Jove, the woman had quite the set of lungs on her. Why would I have killed her though?"

"Because she was linked with you and then moved on to Tomas with an eager eye on his fortune."

"Well now—"

"Did Bettina leave Stroud for you, or the other way around?" Violet interrupted.

Algie squeaked once more. "I...how...what? This isn't quite the thing, you know, Vi. Improper."

"She was a viper, Algie. You are well out of it. You want a wife, but you wouldn't have wanted Bettina Marino for much after she had you bound to her."

Algie nervously glanced at Jack. "You know I do want a wife. Settling down seems to be a good idea. Wouldn't have married *Bettina* though. I mean...no. Even if she weren't a screecher, no."

"How does Violet know you want to marry? And why not Bettina?"

"He offered to take me off of Victor's hands and help me out with my fortune," Violet replied.

Algie winced and glanced apprehensively at Jack. "Listen now. Why not me? I'm a good fellow. Keeps the money in the family. All that. Probably what Aunt Agatha wanted really."

"Who hasn't offered to marry you?" Jack demanded of Violet. He shoved a hand through his hair. "This doesn't have anything to do with the matter at hand."

Violet wouldn't have answered that question regardless, but a very obvious answer came to her mind. "Algie, where did you really go after you couldn't find Theo?"

"I...I..." Algie was blushing furiously. "I..."

"How do you know he is lying?" Jack asked.

"A lifetime of him lying to me," Violet replied. "He's hiding something."

"Hey now. Rather unkind. Speaking of cats..." Algie looked piteously at her, but she was unmoved.

"We're going to think it was Bettina unless you tell us who it really was," Violet warned him. "Where did you go? Were you by the folly? If not, then where? *Who?* Juliette? Someone else?"

He cleared his throat. "A gentleman doesn't talk." His expression was mulish and Violet knew there would be no tricking him. She'd insulted him, and he wouldn't be persuaded until he'd decided he'd proved his point. She'd seen that particular tilt to his expression too many times.

Whomever he was with would probably answer and the fool would have his alibi. "What about Bettina? Why not marry her? Why were you with her if you weren't serious?"

"This is completely inappropriate. Your brother is a fool to let you run around like this...talking about....these...by

Jove, Vi. By Jove, you're a devil. A cattish devil. A man has needs, Vi." His expression looked for a reaction, but Violet held it back.

In fact, she *just* kept herself from throwing something else at Algie. "Did you ever intend to marry Bettina? That was her goal, wasn't it? She was trying to get one of you to offer for her. Or were you just taking what she was offering?"

He laughed, but his ears were red with his fury as he said, "She was offering. I took what was there. Would I have married her? Of course not. She'd been the round of my friends."

"Did she realize? That you wouldn't marry her? The others as well?"

"Stroud...he was a bit more upset than I'd have thought when she threw him over. He...well...he might have been persuaded. Bettina was a woman that wasn't easy to forget."

Violet scowled at Algie. "It didn't bother you that Mr. Stroud cared about Bettina when she threw herself at you?"

"He knows how it is," Algie said. His red ears and cheeks declared he was lying. Violet was betting that Algie had imagined himself in love with Bettina just as well as Stroud. Because if *Algie* admitted that Stroud was upset, the man must have been furious. Or heartbroken. Or both.

"What about Theo? Did he associate with her as well?"

"Didn't give her the time of day," Algie admitted. "He's more business-minded than that. He was pretty furious when Victor shut him out of the group. You know Tomas's little sister is in her last year of school. The girl's trust is enough to turn many a head."

Violet ignored that last comment and slammed out of his bedroom. She ignored Jack, who followed after.

"Theo is here? The one who left bruises on you at your aunt's house?"

Violet casually tucked her wrist behind her. "Victor threw him out the second we ran into him."

"He's around, though, Violet, and this man has to be angry with you and Victor. It's not safe if he's come creeping around this house with you in it."

"Perhaps," she admitted. "We should talk to..."

Jack shook his head. "Violet, it's midnight. Your friend is fine for now. Go to bed."

"I can't," she said. "I can't sleep for worry about all of this."

"I see." He glanced away. "I will investigate this. I will free your soon-to-be-betrothed. Or are you engaged already?"

"I am not engaged. Nor will I become engaged to Tomas. I don't care for him in that way."

Jack's face was entirely unreadable when he replied, "But he cares for you that way."

She didn't see why that was something they had to focus on. Hadn't she given her answer to Tomas's request for her hand? Why did it have to be what these men were interested in?

Jack glanced at his pocket watch. "Violet, go to your room. Lock your door. It's too late to keep working. I'll see you in the morning."

CHAPTER THIRTEEN

Violet didn't sleep well and when she woke, she dressed quickly. She'd put on a long-sleeved simple dress, stockings, basic shoes, and then after some thought, jewelry around her bruised wrist.

It was too early to go to the breakfast room, and Violet wanted to gather her thoughts before she saw anyone else. There was a magic to journaling that helped to uncover her thoughts. She quickly made her bed because the mess would distract her, and put her things away. When she was finished, she sat down at her desk and pulled out the journal. She started by writing about Victor being angry with her and then Jack's reaction to Tomas.

As she described what happened, she was forced to accept that she would have been upset if she'd seen that episode between Jack and another woman. Perhaps his reaction was justified if there really was the beginning of an understanding between them?

As far as Bettina went, Violet had to admit that if the killer was some random passerby, she would never be able to help find them. Hopefully, Jack would do the work she knew he was capable of and find that kind of killer. If, however, the killer were one of their party—and she guessed he or she was—then Violet *could* help. Could and *would* help. She thought over who they had been traveling with and began to make notes about each of them.

Bettina Marino — The victim. Where had she come from? How had she met the group of friends and somehow persuaded them to bring her along? Did the gentlemen all realize that she'd been teasing if not having a relationship with all of them? Why did they pay her way if they knew? Did they really not recognize she was after their money or was that just part of the game?

Violet tried to remember who she had seen Bettina with. Vi had seen the woman track down Tomas and link them. She was so overt in her attentions that it quite bowled over Tomas, at least, who was rather unsure of what to do with someone who ignored polite conventions.

Bettina had a relationship with Mr. Charles Stroud that she threw over for Algie and then she threw Algie over for Tomas. Did her affections actually belong to anyone or were they all a means to a wealthier end?

ALGERNON ALLYN—Cousin. Wealthy. Thrown over by Bettina for Tomas. Was his pride hurt?

Violet scoffed at the question she'd written out and scratched it out.

His pride was certainly hurt.

Violet sketched on a heart near his name and then put an X through it. She tapped her pen against the page. If Algie truly loved Bettina, certainly his heart had been hurt, and Violet guessed that he hadn't been happy regardless. Algie proposed to Violet the first day in England. He wouldn't have done that if he'd had any hope of Bettina.

Violet tapped her pen against the page again and with a heavy heart wrote out:

TOMAS ST. MARKS — He didn't love Bettina and asked

for help in getting rid of the woman. He didn't have a motive to kill her, but he *had* been having memories of the war that day. Could his nature have changed so drastically when he was lost to his ghosts?

Violet paused in her thoughts again. She didn't want to believe Tomas could have hurt someone, but she was also sure that Jack wasn't lying to her about those who had unknowingly hurt their spouse. What if Tomas hadn't been just seeing his dead? What if he'd been seeing some battle where his friend, his young Ben, had died? What would Tomas have done then?

She continued writing. He admitted to removing the knife from Bettina. His prints would be on the knife. He saw her first. He was alone. He was struggling with terrible memories. He was the easiest answer for who might have killed Bettina, and if there was another killer, that person would know that. Would anyone throw unnecessary suspicion on Tomas? If so, could that be a sign?

Violet hated the truth that her notes showed about Tomas and hoped she was very, very wrong. She had to, however, set aside her love and care for Tomas. And in doing so, she had to admit that it was possible that her good friend had killed that woman.

CHARLES STROUD — ?? He seemed to have been connected with Bettina at some point. He was the one who'd hauled Bettina off of Juliette, which was the last time Bettina had been in the room where the party was being conducted. Her body was, however, found some time later. What had he done with her? What had happened between when he'd pulled her off of Juliette and she'd been found mortally injured? He'd manhandled Juliette—would he have done the same to Bettina? Algie made it fairly clear that Charles had been upset when Bettina moved on from him. How upset.

If a man was thrown over by someone he cared for *and* he

watched her throw herself at his friends instead *and* he was rough with women, could he have killed Bettina?

Violet immediately answered. Yes.

But did he? He seems to have been the first of Bettina's lovers in this party—if he was the killer, why did he wait?

Violet sniffed and considered the rest of the party.

FRANÇOIS BOUTET— dancer with his sister. Somehow got Tomas to provide patronage, at least for a while. Didn't help his sister with Stroud. Was he looking for another patron? Maybe even a long-term supporter through Stroud? Maybe he hoped that Stroud would move on from Bettina to the far lovelier and calmer Juliette Boutet?

Violet would never care for Boutet after seeing him watch his sister as she struggled. If only that made him a killer. Violet wondered if Boutet had been in the room when Bettina attacked Juliette. If so, why hadn't he helped his sister? If not...where had he been?

JULIETTE BOUTET— attacked by Bettina directly before the murder. She was a strong woman. She'd held the enraged Bettina off, a feat Violet wasn't sure she'd have been able to duplicate. She was strong enough to have killed Bettina. But would she have? Why?

Violet shuddered as she wrote the next name.

THEODOPHILUS SMYTHE-HILL — A fiend. He was in town. It would have been possible for him to be on the property. Where had he been? What possible reason could he have to kill her?

Violet twisted her wrist. It was hurting since Tomas had taken hold of it and squeezed too hard. She was very much afraid if anyone saw her bruises, they'd assume that Tomas was capable of far worse. Hopefully, the dress and the bracelets would be enough to hide what had happened.

She just needed Jack to give Tomas a chance. To try to find a different killer. She just needed Jack to not assume that it was Tomas because he seemed obvious. Violet glanced her list over and knew that there was another name that she was certain of, but *where* had Victor been? Why hadn't he been in the room and why hadn't he already said? Why was he so angry last night?

Violet wrote the last name on the list with a pang.

VICTOR CARLYLE. Not the killer. But what was he up to?

She decided she needed to find Jack. It was nearly 8:00 a.m., and she was betting he was either in the house or would be soon. Even before Jack, however, she rather needed to speak with Victor. Violet tucked her journal under her arm and left her bedroom.

The hallway was deserted, and she hurried to Victor's door. She felt very exposed since one of the guests in this hall was almost certainly a killer. She knocked on his door quickly and when he responded she stepped inside.

"I knew you'd be here," he said. He smoothed his jacket sleeves and glanced her over.

They very rarely fought, so it was hard for them to make up. They had so little practice with it. They stood there, like fools, uncertain of how to handle what they were thinking.

Violet spoke first. "Why were you so angry with me last night?"

"You were supporting Jack instead of Tomas." Victor tapped his hand against his leg.

Violet stared at her brother. He normally felt like an extension of herself, but at the moment, she didn't understand him at all. Why did she have to choose between Jack and Tomas? Why couldn't she know Tomas wasn't the killer and yet still feel as though Jack had perfectly good reasons to feel the way he did?

She tried to think of how to convey her thoughts and felt as though words were abandoning her. Finally, she asked, "You know how Tomas talks about Ben?"

"The kid who lied to join the battle? Yeah. He's the worst of the stories."

Violet nodded. "Him."

"What about the kid?"

"What would have happened, do you think, if Tomas's memories were of Ben dying again? What if it seemed like he could save Ben?"

Victor's jaw ticked. "I don't think anything would have happened. Because that isn't the way the memories hit Tomas. You just don't want Jack to be wrong. You love him, so you are blind to him being wrong."

"I would lay a bet with the entirety of my fortune, even now, that Tomas didn't kill Bettina." Violet tucked her hair behind her ear and searched Victor's face. His anger was still present, and she wasn't sure how to get him to leave it be.

"You could have fooled me," Victor snapped.

Her eyes burned with tears. Violet didn't know how to handle him this way. Why was he acting like she was somehow not on Tomas's side? Didn't Victor realize that the whole of yesterday with Tomas and what Jack had seen was poisoning the growing love?

She didn't know how to reconcile that the two people she cared most about were both angry with her—and possibly worse—with each other.

"I need you to be on my side," Violet told him.

He snapped again at her. "Don't cry. It won't get me to abandon my friend."

"What is wrong with you? I have not asked you to do that!"

"And when Jack arrests Tomas?"

Violet began pacing Victor's room, pausing to arrange a stack of papers near Victor's typewriter and to put his cufflinks back in the box. "Jack is investigating because we asked him to."

"He's playing at it. To assuage you."

Violet had to swallow back a shriek of fury and instead answered as calmly as she could. "You know he isn't. Jack is an honorable man. He told us he would investigate as though Tomas was not the killer, and he will."

Victor ran his hand through his hair. "We can't count on that, Vi. Tomas needs us to be on his side."

Violet frowned at her brother. Why was he being like this? Her gaze searched his, and he looked away, but not before she saw the panic in it. The panic and the guilt.

"Sit down," she told him. "I need you, Victor."

His jaw clenched again.

"I want to show you something."

He glanced at her. She knew he read her tone—that he wasn't going to like it—but he sat down. She sat across from him and started pulling off her bracelets. Slowly she revealed the circle of bruises around her wrist.

"Did Jack do this to you?"

She shook her head.

"Who did?" Victor demanded. His hand was careful with hers as he looked at it. "You need to tell me, Vi."

"It was Tomas. While I was talking to him, last night."

Victor's mouth slowly opened, and his gaze searched hers. He was shaking his head, but he knew she'd never lie to him. Not ever.

She took her hand from him and put her bracelets back on.

"I was right there. I would have freed you."

"Jack wouldn't have understood. I couldn't let him see because it would have put Tomas at risk. None of this is our fault, Victor. But it's not Jack's fault either. He was here, someone we know died, of course he'd end up being assigned to this case. Of course, he'd be the one. We're *lucky* it's Jack. If it wasn't, some other investigator wouldn't have any reason to look beyond Tomas. Jack is investigating *because* he's trusting our assessment of Tomas. At least enough to give it a chance."

Victor's mouth snapped shut at that.

Violet shook her wrist before Victor. "These bruises are proof that Tomas can hurt people when he's lost to the memories, and I won't have Tomas not getting a full chance because Jack is enraged. The problem is..." She lifted her brows and waited for Victor to fill in the rest. She knew he saw it.

He leaned forward as he said, "Tomas didn't know what he was doing."

Violet pressed her lips together and nodded.

"Bloody hell." Victor stood, pulled Violet up and squeezed her tightly. "I'm sorry."

Vi nodded against his chest, the panic in her own chest easing. She could get through anything as long as she had Victor on her side.

CHAPTER FOURTEEN

"Where were you? During the party, I mean."

Victor glanced at Violet. "When I warned Theo off of Tomas's house the other day, Theo was furious. He made some threats against you, me, even Algie. I asked the servants to keep an eye out for him. Right after the first couple of dances, Mr. Hull came and found me. Said that one of the daily servants in for the party had seen Theo skulking around. I went to remove him before he could act on those threats he'd made."

"Did you find him?"

He held out his hand. His knuckles were bruised again, his middle one split worse than before, and she was surprised she hadn't noticed it. Emotions were too fraught. They were missing things that would never have passed them by on a different day.

"What if it *was* Tomas?" Victor asked, sounding broken. "By Jove, Violet, I don't think I can see him hang for something he can't remember doing."

"I don't know," Violet admitted. "We asked Jack to trust us and investigate as though Tomas wasn't the killer. I think we need to do the same and keep in mind that it might, perhaps, maybe could have been Tomas."

Victor nodded. "Until this killer is found, you need to be extra careful. You stay with me or one of our people—and that doesn't include Tomas. Not until we're sure."

"I think that John is going to take Gwennie back to London if Jack doesn't object. I am convinced we can get Lila and Denny, however, to stay."

"I'll talk to them about it later," Victor said.

They rose and left his bedroom. The breakfast room contained only Algie. He saw the two of them and laughed nervously. "Been a bit afraid to get comfortable since there is a murderer in our midst."

Algie shuffled his teacup around the table, but he hadn't yet made a plate.

"Tell Victor that you owe Theo money again."

Victor's head tilted and the look he shot Algernon was a nasty one. "This is why Theo was lingering here?"

"I don't owe him that much. Just fifty quid, but I don't have it right now. I don't know why he's still here for the money. It's not like I haven't paid him far more. The fellow should trust me. I'm not going to stiff him."

The breakfast room door opened. Jack and Mr. Hull entered. Jack wore a simple brown suit with a blue shirt under it. The colour set off the tan of his skin and made Violet ache. This was not how their reunion was supposed to go.

"There you are," Jack said.

"Good morning," Violet said to Mr. Hull.

The tension was so thick that Algie giggled nervously.

Victor made Violet a plate while she stretched her neck. She was achy and tired. She wanted to sleep but knew if she lay down, she'd find herself remembering the feel of blood drying on her skin. There wasn't going to be good sleep until this case was solved.

Victor didn't need to explain to her why he was serving

her. He was doing it so she didn't have to put pressure on her wrist. It was kedgeree, toast, and fruit, and Violet tucked in with a bit of relief. If only she could go back to worrying about telling Tomas 'no' to his proposal. It had seemed so stressful, but now...murder was so much worse. Violet asked Mr. Hull for aspirin and Victor followed up with a cup of tea.

Jack's gaze took in everything, but Violet didn't have it in her to try to prevaricate at the moment. She needed to just eat and let the painkillers work on her head.

Jack made himself a plate, sitting across from Violet rather than next to her. She tried, and failed, to not be hurt by his placement.

"Are you ready to tell me where you were during the party last night?" Jack asked Algie.

Algie sniffled. "Well...you know....I..."

"You're a suspect until you speak up, Algie," Violet said softly.

"Is that true?" Algie asked with a bit of a squeak, casting a worried gaze towards Jack.

Jack nodded.

"I'll...I'll...I'll tell Jack when you two aren't around. You don't need to know. Already turn your noses up at me, don't you? I don't need it worse."

Victor ignored Algie, who got up and left before he could get manipulated into explaining where he'd been. The look he cast at the twins said he expected just that. Injured and then longing when he turned to the buffet full of breakfast, but he left all the same.

"Are you well?" Jack asked, his gaze on Victor pouring Violet another cup of tea. The twins looked after each other, but this wasn't normal even for them.

"Just a bit of a headache," Violet said, not quite a lie. "We're all worried about what happened."

"On the surface, the answer is obvious. Your friend Tomas killed the woman."

"And under the surface?" Victor asked.

Violet took the aspirin with her tea and closed her eyes.

"You've been traveling with a clutch of vipers."

Violet didn't bother to reply. She was tired. Her heart hurt. Not just for Tomas but for her. She had fallen in love, and it was all coming apart. She could barely even understand why this was happening. She could feel Jack's gaze on her, but she didn't bother opening her eyes.

"We know," Victor answered. "Tomas knew. Tomas asked Violet to get rid of them. He hasn't been feeling well, so—"

"You mean he has been struggling with his memories of the war?"

"When Tomas came home," Victor explained, "he hid it pretty well for a while. He threw himself into things. Family stuff. His mother passed away during the war but his father and his older brother survived the war, along with his little sister. Tomas was so glad to have time with them. At first, Vi and I just thought he was getting through grieving his mother, you know? Then the flu hit and everyone was getting sick and Tomas lost both his dad and his brother within days of each other. Tomas was suddenly in charge of his family estate when he'd never expected anything of the kind. He and his brother were close. His father too. It was devastating."

Violet shuddered.

"We couldn't reach him after a while. He just disappeared. You have to understand, from the first time I went away to school, Tomas was my best friend. He was my temporary Violet when she and I were in different schools. So, I took Violet with me and we came here to find out what was happening with Tomas. He was a mess."

Violet squeezed her eyes shut. That was a time she didn't want to go back to.

Victor continued. "Violet could reach Tomas when no one else could. She could talk to him, and he'd slip out of the memories."

"Is that why he wants to marry her?"

Victor nodded and Violet glanced away. Jack was utterly expressionless, but she could feel his gaze on her.

"He always thought he loved her," Victor said. "Even when we were little. I'd tell him stories of her, and he was infatuated before they ever even met. Tomas doesn't really love Vi, though. I've seen what it looks like to love. Tomas doesn't care for her in the way he thinks he does. He adores her, but he doesn't love her like a wife. He just wants the peace she brings."

"And you want that for her?"

Violet cleared her throat and finally looked up, watching the two of them.

"No. Not at all. Violet won't be happy marrying for the sake of being married, and Tomas would never be that great of a spouse for her anyway."

"You said you love him like a brother," Jack said. "Don't you care that she can help keep him away from his ghosts?"

"It's complicated," Victor said. "Tomas is complicated. But, no. Very simply, no. Violet's wants are more important to me than Tomas's wants. If Violet told me she was going to marry Tomas, I'd do my best to talk her out of it. The good news, however, is that Violet has never needed my help to know what she wants. It's usually the reverse, in fact."

"Why did you call them a nest of vipers?" Violet asked, finished with talking about possibly marrying Tomas with the only man she could imagine marrying.

"I don't like them," Jack said simply. "I've talked to them. That's all it takes. Not one of them told me the complete truth. Each of them could have done it. I'm not sure anyone was actually attending the party, Violet. Even you weren't, Victor. Where were you?"

Victor held out his hand to show Jack the split knuckles. "I was helping Theodophilus Smythe-Hill re-evaluate why he was unwelcome."

Jack frowned. "How long did that take?"

"Long enough to make him hurt, then haul him back to the auto, deposit him inside, send a servant for my man, Giles, and send Theo to London."

"London?" Jack demanded.

Victor nodded. "Algie admitted to me that Theo had made some threats against Violet. He said the same to me. Therefore, Theo can't be near Vi. I wasn't going to risk her out of some misguided attempt to be forgiving."

Jack nodded. "So you were with Theo until your man showed up and then you were with Giles."

"Then I saw a girl running out of the house. She was crying. I heard her say something about blood, and I went running in. What if something happened to Violet? I found her covered in blood. I took her up to her room, stayed until Beatrice was with her and Violet was starting to act normally. Then I found you with Tomas."

The door to the breakfast room opened and Mr. Hull stepped inside once more.

"I had the servants bring breakfast trays to everyone else. I have your policemen here."

Jack nodded. "They have their orders. If you could facilitate their work?"

"Of course, sir. If I may..." Mr. Hull focused on Violet and then back to Jack. "I have taken care of Mr. Tomas in his episodes since he came home from the war. I've seen him cry, I've seen him scared, I've seen him curl into a ball and rock. But I've never seen him become violent. Not ever. I am certain that Mr. Tomas did not hurt that woman. The worst she had to worry about from my master was him weeping on her shoulder."

Jack leaned back in his seat. "That does help, Mr. Hull. I have your word of honour on that?"

"Yes, sir. You do. But you don't have to take just my word

for it. Mrs. Newstone along with Mr. Tomas's man, Higgins, would all tell you the same."

Violet placed her bruised wrist into her lap. "Do you believe Mr. Hull?"

"I was upset last night," Jack said. "I was upset about all of it. When I got to my father's house, I told him about what you said. He told me to man up. To recognize you as the honorable people we know you are. Honorable people don't keep a killer out of prison because they love the person. You loved Meredith, and you helped catch her."

"Man up?" Violet asked, and then the absurdity of it hit her all at once and she giggled. Both Jack and Victor stared at Violet as she laughed, but she couldn't stop. She laughed until she wept. "You're ridiculous."

"You are the one crying and laughing at the same time, darling," Victor said.

"I like your father," Violet told Jack.

"He likes you as well."

She grinned and wiped away a tear. "Tell Jack everything while I eat. Though that laugh...it did help my head feel better."

Victor took Vi's journal and flipped to the last pages as he explained the things that Violet had noted about those staying in the house. Victor added his own thoughts as he discussed Violet's, and Jack took notes. It made Violet feel very useful to have helped.

Victor finally cleared his throat, blushing as he said, "Bettina wasn't the only one who tried to...ah....well...Juliette... both of them seemed to be willing to throw themselves at anyone who was rich enough to set them up."

"Juliette attempted to catch your interest?" Violet asked.

"Honestly, it was a bit like being a fox during the hunt," Victor said. "She made it apparent that she wouldn't say no. When you add in Bettina's pursuit and Violet being distracted, I was utterly defenseless. I felt a bit like Vi, honestly. That inheritance and the fact that she's rather charming really brings out the hounds to chase my Vi."

"Enough about me," Vi snapped. "Juliette Boutet was pursuing you? Those siblings are good at how they manipulate people into paying for them. They got Tomas to pay for them even though he didn't even like them very much."

"Siblings?" Jack asked.

The twins both nodded, glancing at each other and back at Jack.

He shook his head. "Well. Yet another inconsistency. I didn't like how they were answering my questions. So I requested their identification. They're not brother and sister. They're married, which they didn't tell me when I questioned them. I didn't ask them anything other than why they were here. To dance, they said. Now that I think back, they *were* careful in what they said. I might not have realized that they'd been playing siblings if you hadn't said anything."

Violet had paused as Jack spoke, a sip of tea in her mouth. She swallowed it hastily and told Victor, "That does make Juliette's pursuit of you rather mercenary, doesn't it? What a terrible life for them."

Jack nodded, but it was Victor who laughed. "Tomas cannot be trusted alone. Look what happened when we started avoiding him."

"I can't handle being his security blanket," Violet told Victor, but she saw the gleam of interest in Jack's eyes as she admitted, "I don't think I can do that long-term. We need to figure something else out for Tomas."

Victor tossed back the last of his tea. "I've been thinking on that, dear one."

Violet raised a brow. Jack was glancing between them without a word.

Victor set down his teacup and pushed his plate away. "You are right about Isolde. She's the softer version of you. You are too much of a handful for Tomas. The way your mind bounces about would leave Tomas a crumpled wreck. But Isolde—she'd focus on him. She'd enjoy talking him out of his memories. She'd monitor him like a mother hen and probably keep him from ever really descending into the madness. Being desperately needed like that would make her happy."

CHAPTER FIFTEEN

"What possible purpose could the Boutets have for manipulating their marriage like this?" Violet asked. The memory of François Boutet watching Juliette struggle in the arms of Charles Stroud was bothering Violet more than she could say. "Surely it isn't worth the price it costs them?"

"François uses his wife to get money out of people. By Jove, Violet," Victor said, "you know it was why he didn't help Juliette when Charles Stroud was grabbing her. You just don't want it to be true."

Violet nodded, tracing a pattern on the breakfast table. She was a little surprised no one else had come down for breakfast, but when she thought further, she realized that people were trying to keep their secrets safe by hiding away. Or perhaps they stayed away to keep themselves safe since one of them had certainly killed Bettina.

"Is there no chance that the killer was some passerby or indigent? The folly has a roof. Perhaps they took shelter there and were surprised by Bettina in her rage?" Violet knew she was looking for the killer to be someone else. Not out of love for any of their party but because it was just easier to accept a murderous man in the bushes rather than a murderous friend in the house. One was far more sinister than the other.

Victor took Violet's hand and shook his head.

"We will, of course," Jack said, "ensure to the best of our ability that wasn't the case, Violet. I rather think you know that someone in this house killed Miss Marino. There are too many undercurrents for a normal house party."

Violet nodded, biting her lip. The last thing she wanted was for some poor person to be strung up for a crime they didn't commit, even if it was less terrifying.

"Let's start with Mrs. Boutet," Jack said. "Though irregular, I will allow you to stay during questions, so you can help me identify the lies. That will be the quickest way to cut through this."

Violet got a second cup of tea while they waited for Juliette.

When she came in with François, she said, "I hope you don't mind if François is with me? I fear I am a bit nervous after losing poor Bettina."

Jack stood with a polite smile. "I am afraid that I cannot allow that. Everyone will be questioned separately and kept separately until I have spoken with all of you. I have discovered a pile of lies that I must sort out."

"I will not allow you to—" François started furiously.

Jack cut in with a sharp shake of his head. "You will cooperate. You and your wife." The emphasis was on 'wife.' Both of the Boutets leapt in their skin. Jack hadn't said anything about their marriage the night before and had no reason to know that they'd been lying to the others.

François was a hard man. He didn't turn a hair at the implication, but Juliette glanced at him with fear. Her husband, not the police. She was in trouble and probably had been, Violet thought, since she'd met François Boutet.

Jack opened the door and called out. "Come Haversby, take Mr. Boutet to another room alone. Stay with him."

Jack's voice was chilled as he spoke. "Mr. Boutet, let me remind you that a woman has been killed and that you were in this house under false pretenses. You are at the top of my suspect list."

Jack closed the door with a precise click and then sat down across from Juliette.

"You are in trouble, Mrs. Boutet," Jack said clearly and coolly. Violet shuddered at the tone. She hadn't heard that tone from Jack, ever, directed at her. Perhaps they'd been on the path to fall in love longer than she'd realized if he'd been gentler with Violet than he was being with Mrs. Boutet. "Are you going to allow us to help you get out of that trouble?"

Mrs. Boutet was all fine lines in her body and smooth golden hair. It was held back from her face with a hairpin just above her ear. The bob showed off her swan neck, but it was her creamy skin with flushed cheeks and her lips bruised from biting at them that made her seem like a doll come to life. She gazed up at Jack with cornflower blue eyes and then down at her hands, shuddering. Her fists were clenched in her lap and she didn't speak.

Violet thought Mrs. Boutet looked rather like a beautiful, but beaten, dog. The sight infuriated Violet. With a demand she didn't know was coming, Violet asked, "Why don't you leave him? You could divorce him. How can you allow him to make you his...his...whore?"

"I..." Juliette glanced up at Violet and back down at her hands. "You don't understand. I can't survive alone. I..."

"Yes, you could," Violet said. "You are one of the most beautiful women I have ever seen. It would be easy for you to find someone like Algie, someone dumb and gentle, to take care of you."

Juliette shook her head, staring at her hands. She finally whispered, "François would never let me leave him."

"Do you want to?" Violet's voice was even, but she wasn't able to hide the absolute bewilderment.

"I can't," Juliette said, meeting Violet's gaze. "He'd kill me. I'm not like you. Adored and willful. I never had someone like Mr. Carlyle looking out for me. I...this...I have always been helpless against François. I believed his lies when I was young and I have been trapped ever since. Women like you—spoiled and loved—you could never understand."

"Isn't it funny what money can do," Violet said with a sudden inspiration. "It would be so easy for you to go to America. Sneak away and leave."

Juliette bit her lip and shook her head. She was shaking again. "He'd never let me. He'd find me. There's nothing I can do. I will be with François until he is done with me. Which will be when I have nothing left to give."

Jack and Victor were staring at them in shock. Men didn't understand this kind of thing. They never did. Good men like Jack and Victor, who were used to things being a certain way and the kind who only associated with those who would never treat a woman this way—they didn't realize that mothers had been whispering to their daughters to choose carefully. Choose wisely. Careful, wise, or repent at leisure.

"I object," Violet said. She glanced at Jack and Victor and then back at Juliette. "You are not chattel. Women are not chattel. We make our own choices. Make a different choice."

"I did make my choice," Juliette shot back. "As a stupid girl! I wasn't even seventeen. I made a choice and now I am paying for it."

Violet sniffed. She could see that Jack and Victor were both horrified by what Juliette was saying. It would be easy, Vi thought, for Juliette to manipulate either of them.

"I have a lot of money," Violet said, "Too much really."

"Well, isn't that nice," Juliette snapped.

"Enough to make you disappear and give you a start. Pick a place."

"If I tell you François killed Bettina? Protect your precious

Tomas? I won't lie. I have some honour left. Not much, but some."

"I would have helped you before all of this," Violet told Juliette. "There is no price beyond honesty."

"And if I tell you that Tomas killed Bettina?"

Violet sighed. "You know you would be lying. Tomas walked off his memories. He stumbled across Bettina."

Juliette sighed and then carefully asked, "How can I trust you?"

"What you need—the ability to disappear—that would be easy for me. All it really takes is money, of which I have buckets and buckets. You're a caged bird. Time to fly the coop."

Those cornflower blue eyes were searching Violet's face. Desperate to find a lie, to find the truth, to see beyond maybe—to see inside of herself. Could she do this? Could she save herself? And would she?

"What do you need to know?"

Violet barely kept back a crow of triumph. "Why were you here?"

"Charles Stroud," Juliette said. "We've known Bettina for a while. Long before any of us knew Mr. Stroud or Mr. Allyn or Mr. St. Marks. Bettina came to François. She knew how he used me."

Violet shuddered. She couldn't imagine living the life Juliette had been living, but to have others—people like Bettina—see what was happening to Juliette and then...then...giving François marks for Juliette.

Juliette's gaze was fixed on her hands again, so she didn't see their reaction. Maybe she'd seen it before, though, and she knew to look away? Her voice was a mere whisper as she spoke. "Bettina suggested that I target Charles since she'd moved onto Algie. She thought she could get Algie to marry her. She invited us to a party where they'd all be. She wanted me to distract Charles to give her a *righteous* reason to throw Charles over and throw herself at Algernon."

"Why did François allow that?"

Juliette bit her lip. "He wanted me to get Charles to offer to marry me. Bettina laid it all out for François. He bought it all. Decided before we'd even met them that we'd be able to get good money from Charles. Maybe even live off of Charles for years. Charles is a rich man. With the right setup, François was sure we could steal him blind. I...I...think he'd have actually let me marry Charles."

Violet reached out and took Juliette's hands. "I will help you get away. This part of your life can be over."

"Why did Bettina attack you?" Jack asked, using the same gentle tone Violet had acquired. They both were speaking to Juliette as if she were a wild, wounded bird.

Juliette bit her lip. "She told Charles about me. How it was all an act. That I just wanted his money. He was furious. He was so angry. That was when you saw him grab me." She glanced up at Violet. "I thought he might kill me, and Bettina hadn't even told Charles the worst of it—that I was married. She'd only told him that it was all an act. She made herself a victim. She said we knew something about her and we'd blackmailed her to leave him."

Juliette wiped a tear away. "He was squeezing so hard. I thought he might have killed me if he hadn't found me in the hall. If he'd had me alone...well...it would have been so much worse."

Violet barely hid her disgust. "So Bettina realized that Tomas would never offer for her and saw that Victor was disinterested?"

"She tried," Juliette whispered, "To get Mr. Allyn to propose and he laughed at her. Said he'd never marry someone who whored herself to all his friends. There was only Mr. Stroud left. She had to have him back or she'd be out on her ear, and she was desperate. There was quite the row between her and François when she told him we had to move on or she'd reveal it all."

"What," Jack asked as Victor gave Juliette a cup of tea, "did François tell you to do?"

"Deny everything, cry pretty tears, and let Mr. Stroud have his way with me if it would calm him down. He told me to beg, plead, throw myself at him, and swear that Bettina was lying and was jealous. To fix it." The last three words were bitter indeed.

Violet was sick. "Did you?"

Juliette nodded slowly. "I tried. He believed Bettina. Believed that we'd chosen him to mark him. Said I'd always been too eager. I think I could have said or offered him anything and he'd have still wanted to wring my neck. I told François so, and he said if I didn't fix it, he'd be wringing my neck instead."

"So Bettina repented. Threw herself at Charles again. Told him...she was sorry? That she loved him?"

Juliette nodded as Violet laid it out, trying to understand.

"She must have tried to make amends with him and finagle herself back into his arms. Perhaps she told him that she let her need for security blind her to the needs of her heart."

"I'm not sure," Victor said, finally joining in, "that Charles has much of a forgiving or trusting heart. Always was a cold fish."

Violet rubbed her brow. "I don't understand why Bettina didn't realize Charles was rich."

Juliette shook her head. "She knew he had money, but he doesn't wave it about like Algernon does. When she realized that Charles was far more wealthy than Algie and that she wasn't going to get anywhere with Tomas, she was furious. She said she'd been meanly tricked."

Violet's laugh was not amused.

"She's right, Vi. You and I know Charles is wealthy. We've

met his family, seen his home. But, why would an outsider? He always acts like he's a bit pinched."

Violet had never thought about Charles that way or his money at all, so she supposed she wasn't the best judge. "Does Charles know you're married to François?"

"I don't think so."

Violet looked up at Jack. She was sick, but she didn't have any more questions. Not at the moment.

"Mrs. Boutet," Jack said, "I am going to have you put in a new bedroom. Beatrice, Violet's maid, will stay with you."

She nodded and slowly rose. Juliette turned to Violet. "Will you really help me?"

"I will. Anywhere you want to go. A new start. I can do nothing less."

"I'll let you know where."

CHAPTER SIXTEEN

"That is horrifying," Victor said after Juliette walked out. "How does he do that to her? Why would you do that to your wife? She should be the most precious person to him in the world."

Jack rose and paced around the table while Violet pulled out her journal and took notes about what they'd heard. She wasn't even all that surprised anymore. She remembered that cold look on Mr. Boutet's face as he watched Juliette try to escape the furious Charles. Mr. Boutet was a monster in a nice suit.

"It *is* a motive for Charles," Jack said. "And François. Either of them had reason to kill Bettina after that. What a viper she was."

"If Bettina actually knew about Juliette and François being married," Victor said, "she might have threatened them to back off or be revealed. I'm not sure that Mr. Boutet could be counted on to back off."

Violet placed her hand against her chest. She felt suffocated on behalf of Juliette. On behalf of women. She had to make herself take in slow breaths and stop imagining how horrible it would be to fall in love when you were too young to make such big life decisions and then repent for the entirety of your life.

She played with her teacup and tried to clear her mind. Just a little of her bruise was peeking through the bracelets and her long sleeve. Violet herself was hiding, having been hurt by a man in her life. Why did women do this? Understand, forgive, and hide what had been done to them? Was Violet just like Juliette? Better circumstanced because the men in Vi's life, at least, were honorable and good?

She could see it so easily when she thought too hard about it. It was what had happened with Tomas but on a grander scale. Violet knew Tomas hadn't intended to hurt her. So, Violet concealed and protected. Maybe Juliette made excuses too?

She rubbed her fingers over her mouth. "Let's lay out our instincts about what we know so far. What does your gut tell you?"

"You mean like Bettina Marino was killed by someone she knew?" Jack asked.

Violet nodded, turning her teacup on the saucer.

"Neither Algie nor Tomas killed Bettina," Victor declared.

Violet ran her fingers down her list of suspects. "And Juliette. Juliette had motive, she was physically strong enough, but she's been tormented by that animal she's married to. She could have done it. But she didn't."

Jack nodded as he said, "I agree. You aren't going to be in here, Violet, when I question François. I don't want you to catch his attention. But...you could ask Tomas about what we heard here. How did Bettina find out about Charles's wealth?"

Violet nodded and Victor said, "I'll go with her. You don't need me, old man."

Jack cleared his throat. "Will you be going with her because of that ring of bruises on her wrist?"

Violet set her wrist in her lap, glancing between them.

Victor looked sick as he stared to where Violet had hid her bruise away. Jack, on the other hand, looked furious.

Violet sighed. "Why do you have to be so observant?"

Jack was frowning ferociously as he rounded the table to loom over her. She would not squirm, she told herself. A promise that was nearly impossible to keep when Jack asked Victor, "May I have a moment with your sister?"

Victor carefully didn't look at her, the fiend, when he left. Her gaze narrowed on his retreating back, but Jack sat next to her and caught her attention. He searched her face, and then he slowly took Violet's hand in his. He was so gentle as he turned her hand over so the back of her hand was laying on his palm. Carefully, he pushed up the bracelets to examine her bruises. "I can't tell you how much it bothers me that you got these while I was standing right there."

She bit her lip and then admitted, "I didn't want you to know."

He nodded once. "I don't know how to feel about you not asking me for help."

"You and Victor were fighting with each other. Tomas was in his personal hell. He couldn't handle another dust-up. Getting a little bruise seemed the least of my problems."

Jack wasn't appeased. Not even close, but he followed her reasoning. The anger on his face was a little frightening, but she refused to be cowed.

Finally, he said, "You're important to me, Violet." He sounded chagrined, as though he wasn't quite sure what to do with her because of that and wasn't necessarily pleased.

She licked her lips, surprised by how calm she felt. She put her other hand under Jack's, turning the one on his palm until his hand was clasped in both of hers.

"You are important to me as well," Violet said. She, at least, was not upset to know what her feelings were. She knew exactly why he affected her—she was in love with the great oaf.

"I suppose you can understand why I find that hard to believe," Jack said, "since you left for a short time with Isolde and didn't come back for months, and then when I found you again, you're with a man who wants to marry you."

Violet squeezed his hand and let it go. She would not apologize for having other people in her life who mattered as well. "You aren't the only person in my life, Jack. This isn't the time. Let's find the killer, free Tomas, and throw him at Isolde."

Jack snorted. "You think someone would take Isolde over you? Your plan is destined for failure."

Violet's laugh was truly humorous. "She's sweeter, kinder, and less obstinate. She's classically lovely. The only thing I have over Isolde is money, and she's not as poor as her mother acts. Most people would choose Isolde over me."

Violet stood and she glanced down at Jack. He stood with her. "Later. We'll discuss this further later."

She nodded.

CHAPTER SEVENTEEN

Victor was in the hall when Violet exited, and he held out his arm. "Are you unscathed, beloved?"

"Absolutely fabulous, darling twin." It wasn't a lie so much as a refusal to assess how she felt after that little interaction. She supposed there was a ray of hope. When she'd entered the room she didn't have much of that. But she also was sure that Jack had mixed feelings about where they stood as well. "Let's go find out more terrible things to ruin our view of the world and make us wish to retreat to the seaside to be cleaned by the wind and sun."

Victor snorted. "We're going *home*. No more house parties. No guests if we can help it. Our trusted servants and each other. No need to fear a knife in the back."

They went to Tomas's room and his man opened the door. He was a little man, dapper with a bald head and sharp eyes.

"We need to speak with Tomas," Victor said.

The man hesitated until Tomas shouted, "Let them in, Higgins."

Tomas was sitting next to the fire, book in his lap but

staring at the flames. He wore one of those large robes lined and too warm for the weather, but Tomas seemed cold. He shivered while they watched. When he spoke, it was with a hoarse voice. "Lewis Carroll was a genius."

"Why's that?" Victor crossed and sat across from Tomas, patting the arm on his chair for Violet.

"We're all mad here," Tomas said and then laughed, but there was nothing in that sound that was amused. "I killed Bettina. It's the only thing that makes sense."

Violet stood and kicked Tomas in the shin, swift and hard.

"Ouch!"

"Never," Violet said furiously, leaning into his face, "say that again. Never!"

"Vi, I..."

"Never," Vi said. "Never. They'll take you at your word. They'd have to. You did *not* kill Bettina. You are not that kind of man. You worry about that inside of your head and don't let a peep of it cross your lips."

Tomas grabbed her forearm. Victor rose quickly but before he could say a word, Tomas gently moved her bracelets. "I hoped this was one of those terrible memories that aren't real." Tomas shuddered at the bruises on Violet's wrist. "By Jove, Vi. I'm sorry. I...holding you made me feel safe. I held too tightly. What if I did something like that to Bettina? I could have killed her. It could have been me. Look what I did to you."

"Don't be an idiot," Victor said. "Violet will kick you again."

"Have you eaten?" Violet demanded, ignoring the apology.

"Uh-oh," Victor laughed. "Violet's gone into caretaker mode. Tomas, you did not kill Bettina."

Violet rose and crossed to Higgins. "Bring Tomas food, please."

"He won't eat, my lady," Higgins said. He looked over Vi's

shoulder at Tomas and his worry was evident. For such a little man, he seemed to loom with the cloud of his concerns.

"He will," Violet said, scowling at Tomas.

Mr. Higgins grinned at Violet. "Yes, my lady."

Violet returned to her perch next to Victor. "Bettina deliberately pulled in Juliette and François to distract Charles while she went after Algernon. Bettina thought that Algie was wealthier than Charles. Why?"

"It's a game he plays." Tomas sounded exhausted. "To see if people will choose him for him. He almost married a fortune hunter once. He's been angry ever since. He says I'm a fool. I should hide what I have so that people don't try to take advantage. He's been needling me about Algie and Theo, let alone the Boutets and Bettina. Tomas the fool. Tomas the schmuck. You know what he's like, Victor."

"So," Victor said, further explaining to Violet, "Charles lives cheap, talks like he's hurting, asks people for random fivers. It's ridiculous. He's got more ready cash than nearly everyone I know except for you and Tomas."

Violet glanced at Tomas. "Bettina failed Charles's test. She didn't stay with him without the money. She, who had nothing, didn't find what little she thought he had, good enough."

Victor was furious. "People are so worried about money. Having it. Not having it. Who has more? Algie is wealthy compared to the vast majority of mankind. He has a good allowance. He doesn't have to work. He'll inherit well enough to not ever have to work. And yet, he's jealous of me and Vi. Is his life so hard because he isn't disgustingly wealthy? If he only knew how much work it was for Violet to manage that business."

Tomas stretched his legs out. "Algie talks about it all the time. How it wasn't fair that the inheritance went the way it did."

"It wasn't fair," Violet agreed. "Aunt Agatha could have been far more equitable. What else do you know?"

Victor glanced at Tomas, who seemed truly upset as he said, "That man who was yelling last night is the one you love. Why do you love him? He seems a beast!"

Violet grinned cheerily as though she wasn't worried that Jack would decide she wasn't worth the trouble. Or that Tomas was extremely upset. "What does that have to do with anything?"

"I don't know. I thought he'd be different than he seems to be. Maybe less of an ogre."

"He's a good fellow," Victor said. "You'd like him if you weren't a jealous blighter. As for Jack? Meeting you while you clutched Violet, making her bloody and you lost to the ghosts wasn't the best start, my friend. Jack is swimming in jealousy. He's having to realize he is jealous. It's a bitter pill. He's choking on it."

Tomas laughed bitterly. "I'm going to enjoy that, if it's all right with you."

Violet ignored both of them and asked, "Did you tell Bettina that Charles was wealthier than Algie?"

Tomas shook his head., "You know who would have done that? Algie."

Violet thought about that and realized she could imagine such a conversation perfectly. Algie petulant and upset when he realized Bettina was all mercenary. If Algie figured out that Bettina was purely driven by avarice instead of love? Algie could be petty.

Tomas glanced as Violet paced his rooms. He had a sitting room outside of his bedroom, so there was a couch, two chairs next to the fire, a desk. With doors leading to a bath, his bedroom, and another room, his rooms were extensive. The way Tomas was curled in on himself left him looking a bit like a child playing at being the man of the house.

Mr. Higgins came back with a tray for Tomas and tea for them all. Violet asked him to go and get Algie.

When Tomas hesitated to eat, Violet said, "Eat or we'll hold you down and shovel it in your mouth."

He glanced at her and laughed. While Tomas ate, Violet read *Alice in Wonderland* to him until Algernon appeared.

"Oh, by Jove," he said as he appeared, "you've got a bit of the nosh. Been dying for some toast and eggs, but these two drove me out of the breakfast room."

Tomas shuddered.

"Are you a complete nincompoop, Algie?" Violet chastised. "Why would you say that? This isn't a joke."

"She was stabbed in the front," Tomas said, sounding haunted. "Right above her left breast."

Violet shuddered and Victor smacked the back of Algernon's head. "Well, Algie, was it you?"

"Who killed Bettina?" he gasped. "Well now, I see how it is. You've turned on me, your own blood, your family. For Tomas. Trying to pin this murder on me? That is hardly fair. Rather evil to be honest."

"No," Victor growled. "You idiot. You don't think Tomas killed Miss Marino either, sit down and eat. Did *you* tell Bettina that Charles is wealthier than he puts on?"

Algie gasped again, holding his hand to his chest. "Why would you say that?"

"Because none of us did, and somehow she found out. Tomas didn't. The Boutets didn't know. Was it Charles who revealed himself, or did you?"

Algie blushed furiously. "Well now. Been talking about me, have you? Assuming I'm the fool."

Violet took a sip of her tea and said blandly, "He was the one who told Bettina."

"Vi!" Algie squeaked. "Vi! Why do you say such things?"

"We don't think you killed Bettina, Algie. We all know you too well for that. But you told her, didn't you? It led to her death. It must have."

Algie's blush was so deep and fiery that Violet thought she

might be able to warm her fingers against his cheeks. “She was a catty woman. She, well, I didn’t think she was really moving on from me to Tomas. Only she did. She threw me over. I hadn’t understood until she told me she was done. I didn’t understand she had no idea about how wealthy Charles is. I thought she left him for me because she’d fallen in love.”

Violet held back her scoff. Algie had been flattered that Bettina had seemed to pick him. So when he got thrown over too—his pride had been hurt. Possibly his heart, but certainly his pride. It was *just* like him to lash out when he realized how it played out.

Violet could understand, and she didn’t hate him for it. Instead, she took his hand. “Algie, you are too good for this. And for that woman. You have a lot to offer a woman. You don’t need to buy one with your fortune or…”

Algie shook his head, giggling a little meanly. “Victor and Tomas always steal the hearts of anyone I am interested in. The girls like me all right until they meet my friends. Richer, smarter, more handsome.”

She’d have felt bad for him if she wasn’t so inured to his whining. She just patted his arm and glanced at Victor, who knew her so well, he was biting back a laugh.

“You don’t have anything to whine about, Algie. At least you’re not mad as the hatter,” Tomas snapped. “I’m having a hard time feeling bad for you, you…you…spoiled blighter!”

“I think you told Higgins to read Tomas the wrong book, Vi.” Victor crossed his legs. “All that talk of madness is striking too close to home.”

“Well, shouldn’t it?” Tomas asked. “She dreamed and didn’t know it wasn’t real. I dream. Unable to tell the difference between what is real and what is not. At least Alice was a little girl incapable of harming anyone.”

“Clearly,” she said dryly to Victor, ignoring Tomas’s outburst.

She rose and straightened Tomas’s desk. As she worked

she considered what they'd learned. "Were you aware that Juliette and François Boutet are married?"

"What? Where are their spouses? Someone has been telling you fairy stories, luvie," Algie said. "That Juliette has been after Charles since the day they met. Paved the way for me and Bettina to be honest. No married man would put up with that. Or a brother of a married sister. He'd have taken her aside and told her to be true. Any man would have."

Victor and Violet glanced at each other and Victor shook his head slightly. Don't tell Algie that the relationships had been planned before they'd even begun. It was the kindest route.

Tomas, on the other hand, understood immediately. "They don't look alike, do they? They pretended to be siblings because it made finding patronage easier."

"François Boutet is a snake in the grass," Victor said. "I have never been more appalled at a member of mankind, barring murderous cousin Meredith."

"Well, she did kill our aunt," Algie said idly. He didn't even sound upset. Violet crossed to him and smacked his shoulder. "What, Vi? Goodness, Merry did. Of course, she's the worst of us."

Violet smacked him again. "Don't say it like that. Like it's half a joke. It's not." Vi had to bite her lip to keep back shouting at him. "Nothing about her death is funny. Nothing about Bettina's death is funny. This is all disgusting."

"Speaking of things that aren't funny," Victor said to Algie, "you have to stop associating with Theodophilus. He threatened you to me. But far more importantly, he threatened Violet."

Algie sniffed. "Well now. I...I don't appreciate any part of this...this...this setup! You all are uniting against me."

"Let me be perfectly clear, Algie. You're our cousin. We care about you. I paid your debt to Theo yesterday when I sent him to London. If you'd told me you needed help, I'd have helped you with him."

"You sent him to London?" Algie asked. "Well, I'm not sure that's quite the thing. I... That was poorly done, Victor. Theo's a good enough fellow."

"Then you won't be happy with my next statement. If I see you with Theo again or if I see you helping Theo into our group, or needing money because you fell for Theo's tricks, or if you bring Theo anywhere near Violet again. Ever. We're done."

"Done? What does that mean?"

"You know exactly what it means." Victor lifted a brow, but the set to his jaw was telling.

"I...well...I...don't think that's quite fair. Tomas? You don't agree, do you?"

He cleared his throat. "Victor gave me an idea of what Theo did to Violet."

"She was teasing him. She overreacted. Theo's a good fellow. Been a friend a long time. We all need to just calm down, now."

Victor stood, leaning over Algie. "Of the two, I choose Vi. Make your own choice but realize there are consequences."

"Well I...I...of course, I choose you. Violet, this isn't quite the thing. Surely you see..."

Violet bit the inside of her mouth until she could taste blood. How dare he say she didn't understand? That she didn't realize Theo's intent? How dare Algie demand that she pretend all was well? She wouldn't feel like she could leave Victor's side if Theo were around.

"Violet, don't say a word," Victor said, touching her shoulder. "It doesn't matter what Violet thinks. Not when I'm concerned for her safety."

"Her safety?" Algie laughed, a nervous squawk.

"Make a choice, Algie. Drop us a note. When we leave

here, I want to hear you're done with Theo—who manipulates your money out of you—or I want to hear that you've chosen him, and we're done with you. It's a simple either-or situation. But if you bring him around Vi again, it isn't just Theo who will get a beating."

CHAPTER EIGHTEEN

Violet wanted to go back to her room after they'd spoke with Tomas. The need to apologize to Gwennie and Lila was distracting Violet from nearly all else. She had been fighting with both Victor and Jack and had snapped at her friends. She expected better of herself.

If she'd had Beatrice, she'd have sent her maid for them. Violet was sure she had the bigger bedroom and better space to linger, but Beatrice was keeping Juliette safe. Violet dug through her trunks until she found one of the bottles of limoncello she'd brought with her to Bruges and three of the smaller boxes of chocolates. She put all of the things in a basket from the armoire, added her and Victor's more recent book along with the review that had described V. V. Twinning as a female, and carried them down to Lila's bedroom.

Violet had to kick the door since her arms were full, and a moment later Denny opened it. "Thank goodness, Vi. Lila is moping. Save me from her woebegone eyes! She knows I can't take it when she's upset."

"I have chocolates for you and Gwennie," Violet called to

Lila, "and some for me since I have the most sour taste in my mouth after hearing the things I've heard this morning."

"Uh-oh," Denny said. "Gwennie has been swept off by Davies. I'll take her chocolates. I'd hate to force you two to overindulge." His charming grin made both of them laugh.

Violet held up the bottle of limoncello and his gaze focused on it. He glanced at the clock and then grinned., "I believe we've got a couple of glasses."

Denny worked the cork out of the bottle and poured each of them a glass and then raised it to the ladies. "I'll go for a walk and leave you two to your gossip."

Lila tossed an indulgent glance at Denny. "You want to eat all of those chocolates in one sitting without judgement. Violet, don't be confused by this talk of a *walk*. He'll be finding a corner with a comfortable chair and silence. No doubt he'll leave said chair with chocolate round the mouth and on the fingertips. Somewhere in the world a child is acting like a full-grown man while my husband confuses himself for a child."

Denny adjusted his jacket, grinned at his wife, winked, and escaped with his glass of limoncello and box of chocolates.

The two friends stared at each other before Lila said, "You don't look like you're cracking apart anymore. I assume all is well with Victor again?"

Violet nodded and popped one of the chocolates into her mouth. She admitted, "I was awful last night, I know. I'm sorry, darling."

"Don't worry, Vi. I understood. Anytime you and Victor argue, it's like your world goes awry and you aren't quite yourself."

Violet cocked her head. "Are you ready to hear it all?"

Lila rubbed her hands together with an avaricious glee for the gossip. "Oh, yes. Yes, oh yes."

Violet laughed, handed Lila her own box of chocolates and

threw herself onto the end of their bed as Violet described what she'd learned. She paused for Lila to rage, gasp, and comment at all the best places.

"They're married?" Lila asked. "And he was...was...making her..."

Violet nodded when Lila stopped and they both shuddered.

"You're going to help her leave him. Please say you are. I'll help too. However I can. Maybe we can find him and filet him? Cook certainly has the right kind of knife."

"Of course, I am going to help her," Violet said. "Aunt Agatha would turn over in her grave if I didn't."

"She'd haunt you until you repented then haunt you longer so you learned your lesson well. You know...if she's sure he'll look for her, my sister lives in Lyme. We could send Juliette to Joanna. Jo would help. Juliette could linger there while we get the gentlemen to persuade him to France. They can tell him that they booked her passage and took her to the dock. We could even pay someone to take the journey under her name. Then, when Mr. Boutet is entirely led amiss, Juliette could leave from Lyme to wherever she decides to go."

Violet nodded. "That is a good idea. You and Denny avoid her. If François has no reason to believe that she left with you, his attention will be elsewhere. Juliette doesn't seem to be a creature who frightens at nothing."

"Making her situation all the worse," Lila murmured.

Violet shivered. "Also, when you buy train tickets—buy them for somewhere else and then add on Lyme later. Somewhere busy where they won't notice if you stay for a few days and then move onto Lyme. Maybe even travel separately. If Juliette is afraid, I think she must have reason. Even if she's wrong, I will do her the credit of taking her seriously."

Lila nodded. "Denny and I could use the auto that Victor took when Giles is back and drive her to Lyme. Or at least drive her far enough that we could put her on the train somewhere else where he wouldn't think of looking."

"Maybe we should even disguise her," Violet said. "She is rather eye-catching."

"As you said, darling," Lila said, "if that makes her feel safe, we should do it. We can put a wig on her. Or clothes that make her look large. Easy enough."

Violet sipped her limoncello, letting the flavor pool in her mouth before she asked, "Did you get my letter about Victor's present?"

Lila smirked. "Yes, darling. I found just what you're looking for. You'll be thrilled."

Violet paused. "Why are you smiling like that?"

Lila winked and took a sip of the limoncello and then lifted her glass. "What an odd way to spend a late morning. I was just laughing at us. My mother would take me by the ear if she saw us now. Drinking limoncello and eating chocolates, lying about without one thing to recommend us."

"One of the reasons," Violet laughed, "that you married Denny as young as you did. Escape from the good work your mother expected of you."

Violet flopped back onto the bed and lifted her legs into the air, stretching her toes towards the ceiling. "Aunt Agatha would pour herself a glass of limoncello and make us give up all her favourite chocolates, exchanging them for the lesser ones. My goodness, Lila, I miss her so much it hurts."

"I know you do," Lila said. "I'm sorry you do."

After a long moment of silence, Lila spoke again. "We'll have to go shopping. When we're back to normal. You'll need to find a birthday dress. I was going to suggest you wear that peacock piece of divinity, but I am guessing..."

Violet answered the unspoken question. "I'll never wear it again. I am guessing that Beatrice—magician that she is—will return the dress to its previous state, but it will never touch my body again."

Lila frowned and stood, crossing to her door a moment before someone knocked. She pulled the door back and stared in shock at François Boutet.

"I am looking for Juliette," François said. "You women stick together at times. Tell me where she is. You know, I think."

Violet frowned at him, a rush of fury hitting her as she remembered the sight of the lovely Juliette crying about what this man did to her. She rose and crossed to stand behind Lila, offering her support as she put a hand on her friend's back.

"I don't know where she is," Violet said, feeling a foretelling of the future. She told herself they were safe together, but she felt a flash of fear. He was a cruel man. He was the cruelest to his wife. What would he be to someone he didn't care about at all, someone like Violet or Lila? "Mr. Wakefield had her taken to another room. I wasn't informed of where that might be."

François Boutet's jaw tightened and Violet felt another flash of fear. It deepened as she realized his fists had clenched.

"What did she tell you?" His gaze had narrowed viciously on Violet, and she winced in the face of that undisguised hatred.

"You'll need to discuss that with Mr. Wakefield."

"Why were you in the room? What business did you have there?"

"You'll need to discuss that with Mr. Wakefield," Violet repeated. She clutched at the doorframe and prayed that someone would come along.

Lila grabbed Violet's arm, and Violet could tell by Lila's stiffness that she was afraid as well.

"Don't be spreading lies about us." Mr. Boutet leaned into Violet. "I don't take kindly to liars who think they understand things they don't."

"You'll need to leave."

François smirked at Violet, pressing even closer, and then Victor stepped up behind him. He reached out and grabbed François by the back of the neck, yanking him away from Violet and Lila.

"Hey now! What do you think you're doing? Let go of me, you bedamned animal."

"What am I doing?" Victor snarled. "Telling myself not to be the one who commits the next murder."

"I was looking for Juliette," François squawked. "I did nothing. You are mad, sir!"

Victor did something with his hand that had François gasping, his knees shaking.

"Violet," Victor snapped, "you're starting boxing and jiu-jitsu classes when we get home. You too, Lila. By Jove, men are animals. This one is the worst!" Victor shook François.

Violet glanced at Lila, who grinned at the sight of François struggling under Victor's arm.

"You think I am joking? Wait until I tell Denny who I found outside of this bedroom. He left you here together because he thought you'd be safe." Victor was shouting at that point and Denny, Jack, and two uniformed policemen raced up the stairs.

"I did nothing!" François called. "Help me! He's a madman. I didn't lay a hand on either of them."

"Victor," Jack said flatly, "let him go."

"I have not finished teaching him a lesson."

"Where is Haversby? I told him to keep an eye on this one." Jack glanced back at the policemen and then lifted a brow. One of the policemen peeled off and went jogging down the stairs while Jack said to the other, "Jones. Take this fellow and lock him in a room. Make sure he doesn't get out this time."

CHAPTER NINETEEN

"Lila darling, are you all right?"

"Of course, I am," she said lightly. She'd relaxed the moment Victor had appeared and she grinned at everyone. "That was exciting, wasn't it? I think I'll have some more limoncello. The mix of chocolate and limoncello was brilliant, Vi. You always have been a brainy thing. Never more so, it seems, when it comes to chocolate."

She giggled nervously and stepped back into her bedroom, waving the others in. Denny took her limoncello, drained it, and then said, "You've given me heart palpitations, my love. Your chattering tells me you have them as well. All is well. The bad man is gone, and your useless spouse has returned."

Lila patted Denny on the head and took back the glass to refill it. She sat on the bed next to her husband and crossed her ankles. "Tell us where we're at. Is this murder almost solved? I find I would like to go home."

Jack shook his head, shoving his hand through his hair. "The only prints on the knife that can be identified belong to Tomas. There was a smeared one that we couldn't identify. As far as the suspects, Victor has an alibi. Algie has an alibi. It seems likely that either Tomas killed Bettina unaware of what he was doing or—"

"It wasn't Tomas," Victor said flatly. "Who is left?"

"Charles and François. Charles had nothing useful to add and no alibi. François seems to do nothing but lie. Technically Mrs. Boutet could also be the killer, but I think if she'd been the one, she'd probably have said that François had done the deed and got rid of her fiend of a husband while also escaping a murder charge. She could be the killer, but I don't believe she is."

"She is strong enough," Lila said. "If Miss Marino had attacked me like she attacked Juliette, I'd have been curled into a ball on the floor, covering my head. Juliette held her off. Her slenderness doesn't really convey how strong she must be."

"The most likely choices," Violet said, "are Charles and François. Charles was the one who pulled Bettina off of Juliette. He may well have been the one who pulled her out of the house, manipulated her to the folly, and murdered her there. My only hesitation there is that Charles and Tomas are long-time friends. Killing her when we all knew he was caught in his memories makes Tomas the likeliest suspect. It's a very good cover-up. Cruel and vicious, but effective."

Victor took Violet's glass of limoncello as Jack considered. "That might be why she was killed when she was. How good of friends are Charles and Tomas?"

Violet couldn't answer that, and Victor shrugged. "I don't know, really. We're all school chums, but Charles was never one I was as close to."

"Would he have known that Tomas would go walking like that?"

"I think anyone paying attention might realize that," Violet answered. "It was one of the first things Victor and I realized would help Tomas. He does it almost instinctively now. Anywhere Tomas stays for long, he knows all the walks around him, explores all the places."

Victor nodded. "I've walked hours with him. Given that Tomas has been having a hard time for a while, I would guess that everyone knew that about him."

"And he was doing so poorly at dinner," Lila said. "He seemed to be hanging on Vi's every word, and she was doing that thing she does where she paints memories for him to pull him out of the old ones. He looked like he was drowning."

Violet sighed. "He walked off after that trumpet player tripped, too. It's an easy guess that the loud noise sent him running after seeing him at dinner. It might have sent him running on a good day, let alone a day like yesterday."

Jack nodded. "I'm not sure how we'll identify which of them is the killer. The truth is—all the evidence we've recovered points to Tomas. If it wasn't him, we need a confession. Something irrefutable."

Violet stood and paced while the rest considered options. Neither Charles nor François had an alibi. Both had a motive. Each motive was compelling. Betrayed love for Charles, money for François.

"We need Juliette to help us," Violet said as she stared out the window. "If the killer is François, she might be able to get him to confess. Or to say where he was. If we were listening, we could be the witnesses of his confession. It will be more difficult with Charles. He won't confess to anyone. Not sure that François would either, but we could at least try. She might able to find out enough to get us the next step of the way."

"Let's start with François," Jack said. "We'll work from there. Of the two men, François has shown himself to be unprincipled. And of the two men, François doesn't care what happens to Tomas. Charles might."

Violet nodded, wishing she could believe that Charles cared very much. If only.

"When this is over," Lila said suddenly, "we're having a dinner. Friends only. No underlying tensions. No worries. Just food, drinks, and enjoying ourselves."

Violet leaned back and admitted, "Add cake, and it sounds a little like heaven. I love Isolde and Gerald, but I always felt as though they were...I don't know how to describe it."

"They watched you," Victor said. "Isolde because she wants to be like you. Gerald because he's protective. He's not quite sure what to do with you. I imagine it was suffocating. It was suffocating to watch, to be honest, my dear. You carried on like a wonderful soldier. I don't think Isolde even knew how you felt."

Violet shrugged. "Perhaps suffocated. I certainly felt watched. I don't know. I wasn't comfortable."

Victor grinned lazily at Violet as she paced. "You'd think being rich and spoiled would be easier. Yet murders and machinations abound."

"I suppose we'll have to carry on," Violet said with a grin. "Struggle through somehow."

Jack snorted and Lila laughed, holding out her box of chocolates to the group.

"Violet darling," Victor said as he took one, "how many boxes of chocolates did you buy in Bruges?"

"Perhaps all of them," Violet admitted, returning to pacing. "One can never be fully sure."

Victor laughed. "That seems accurate for you, love."

"Violet," Denny started, "have I told you how I adore you? You've been a sister to me. The true companion of my heart. Who understands my heart...my soul—"

"Yes, Denny, you may have more chocolate."

Lila snorted. "Denny darling, Violet is a sure bet for chocolate. What is also a sure bet is the stone you've lost will come again."

"I'll walk with Tomas," Denny offered. "He needs someone to keep him safe during those times until he's a little better settled. I'll have chocolate and walk with my friend. It will all work out fabulously."

"What happened to your job?" Victor demanded. "Don't you have to appear at the office, bowtie in place, briefcase at the ready?"

Denny grinned. "My beloved Aunt Louisa has passed on to a better place."

Lila smacked him. "Pretend to be sad, my love. Otherwise we'll look like the worst of fiends."

Denny shrugged. "I did care for her. She always had chocolates, speaking of the sweetest kind of women. However, I have to say she was old. I'm not being cruel. She was ready to die. She told me so. Then she told me she knew Lila and I were deliberately not having children. The old dear made me promise to eventually have one or two, told me to be a good boy, and to be kind to my wife. Not sure there could be a better final command than those. I am done working, my darlings. The world is a beautiful place and the next life is better for having someone like her."

"Denny," Violet said, giving him her box of chocolates, "I am sorry about your loss, and to be honest, I am shocked that you have such deep feelings for anything other than food, alcohol, and Lila. That was nearly beautiful."

"Don't be silly, darling," Denny said, taking her chocolates with a kiss on her forehead. "I adore you as well."

Lila laughed. "His love may last through the two minutes it takes him to eat those chocolates as well."

"You all are a bunch of children," Jack complained. "Spoiled children."

Victor snorted. "You knew what we were when you joined us. Violet, at least, is clever. Denny and I are useless. Lila—" Victor cocked his head at her, glancing over her with a quizzical expression. "You fall in between."

Jack sighed. "I have to go speak with Juliette."

"If financial persuasion will get her to help you, I will

cover it," Violet said. "I already feel as though she deserves something more."

Jack shook his head. "She should help you because we're finding a killer. I won't bargain with her."

"You don't have to," Lila said. "It's Violet's horror to end up stuck with the wrong man, a cruel man. Juliette is living Vi's nightmare. Therefore, Violet is incapable of not helping. Incapable of not spoiling the woman. Your care for other women," she said to Violet, "is why I've been reading profiles of families who wish to adopt a baby. It's why you are finding a way to get Ginny to actually go to school. It's why I've been sending care packages to Anna Mathers at school and stopping by to bring her and her friends out to have treats." She faced Jack. "Violet is going to help Juliette whether you like it or not."

Jack turned to Violet, who was blushing a little. "Ginny? The little devil of a girl who helped you find Isolde when she was taken?"

Violet shrugged.

"Helen Mathers? What are you doing there?"

"She's living in Vi's Amalfi villa. Violet is helping to find the baby a home."

"How?" he asked. "Why?"

"She needs help." Violet tucked her hair behind her ear and glanced away. She offered Jack her glass of limoncello to turn his focus elsewhere, but she was unsuccessful.

"She needs help. So you're just helping her?" He wasn't trying to be dismissive. It was as though he couldn't quite understand it.

"So, yes," Violet said. "I'm just helping her."

Victor cleared his throat. "Don't be so baffled, Jack darling." Jack's gaze turned to Victor, who winked. "The fact that Violet is both witty and kind is why she intrigues you, despite her enormous burden of being an earl's daughter and richer than Midas. Fortunately for her, I even out the rest of her negatives."

"I think that's enough, dear Victor," Violet said. "Shall we catch a killer and then escape home? Please? I never wanted to come here in the first place. And I *do* have families to interview and business decisions to make."

"Oh, there she goes again," Denny said, eating the last of Violet's box of chocolates. "Being the responsible one. At least some of our fore-bearers can be happy at where their progeny ended up."

CHAPTER TWENTY

Jack didn't want an audience, but Violet suggested that the easiest place to overhear what was happened between François and Juliette was in the old ballroom. They'd used it often as children, and there were balconies that looked down on the dance floor. And floor-length curtains that would hide someone easily.

"You can't really keep us out," Violet told him.

"I can," Jack said.

"Mmm, you can try. But we'll end up in there anyway. You don't know this house as I do."

Jack shot Violet a dissuading look, but she was unmoved.

"No," Jack said. "That's final. This could be dangerous. You will remain here." He left before Violet could argue.

"So," Victor said the instant the door closed, "the secret passage?"

"Indeed," Violet said. She winked at Lila and Denny, and they waited a few minutes before walking to the library. Violet pulled a latch near the fireplace, and one of the bookcases moved.

"Oh, these old houses. My grandfather had a passage like

this in his house. It made the best place to hide when the nanny was looking for me," Denny said. "Unfortunately, I wasn't very discreet, so eventually I was found out and my refuge was lost to me."

Violet glanced at him and at Victor, who lifted a torch and turned it on. Violet winked at her friends once again and followed her brother into the passageway.

They made their way up a staircase and onto the second level of the ballroom. François and Juliette were already in the room. Violet tiptoed forward after placing a fingertip over her mouth. She would be seen if she remained standing, so Violet dropped to her knees and crawled forward. She peeked over the side of the balustrade and saw Juliette pacing.

"...they ask you?"

Juliette was shaking as she moved. "I...he...knew about us being married. He asked about that. I didn't know what to say, so I admitted it. Said we found it easier to get work as siblings."

"Not about that!" François shouted and slapped her. "About Bettina. Did you tell them we were together?"

Juliette blinked up at her husband, holding her cheek. "We weren't together when she was killed, François."

"You should have lied!"

Juliette backed away and asked, "Did you kill her?"

François cursed at Juliette in French. "Of course I didn't!"

"I slipped out of the party after you left," Juliette whispered. "Charles wasn't there and you weren't there, so I decided to get some air. I ran into one of the maids. She knew where I was during the murder. I couldn't lie about where you were. They already knew otherwise."

François cursed again. "If they find out where I was, I'll be arrested."

"I don't understand," Juliette whispered. "Why? If you did not kill Bettina, why would they arrest you?"

"Our days here were limited once Bettina's scheme went

awry and Charles realized what she was. We don't have enough capital to carry on until we find another patron. Something had to be done. Therefore, I did it."

"What did you do?"

"These fools don't lock their bedroom doors and they leave their expensive trinkets out. They deserve to have them taken."

"François," Juliette said. "They'll think it was us."

"It was us. They'll think it was servants. Don't be stupid. I already targeted that little maid, Mary. The one who kept forgetting to light our fires. I've told the uptight butler that I saw her poking around the rooms. I left the cheapest looking thing in her room under her bed. She'll get taken in and we'll get away."

"So you were stealing from them while Bettina was killed?"

"No, idiot. My goodness, Jules, you're a fool. I was getting rid of the stuff. I met the fence, didn't I? What better time to sneak out and sell the things when everyone thinks we were dancing and drinking in poorly lit rooms? And when the estate is crawling with strangers?"

Violet glanced back at Victor, who raised a brow. She had things stolen and had no idea? It was possible. Though Violet tended to be very careful when she had her jewelry out. Maybe just the others?

"We're leaving," François commanded. "Gather your things. It won't take all that long for them to arrest that idiot, Tomas. They're going to realize I've slipped the room soon. I need to get back."

"Where are we going?"

"I've got a new income for us."

Juliette nodded. "Of course. Of course. Where will we be going?"

François grabbed Juliette's arm and demanded, "Does it matter?"

"Of course it doesn't, my love." Juliette's voice was thick with tears. "You know I'll follow you anywhere. You know that I'll do whatever you say."

François laughed meanly. "You will. And don't you forget it. I've got the golden goose for us. Good times ahead."

Juliette nodded. She slowly straightened as she asked, "François? Please. Where are we going?"

Violet could make a guess. It all came together for her in a flash. But François would never tell Juliette all of it. Not with how he treated her. It was like he enjoyed her pain. Violet stood suddenly, not thinking things through. "I know where, Juliette."

Juliette screamed and François shook her viciously. "What's this? A trap?"

"You met your fence at the folly, didn't you?" Violet placed her hand on the rail and slowly walked down the stairs, watching François abuse his wife. The curtains twitched, and Violet saw one of the policemen peeking out and then sliding back behind the great drape of fabric.

François shouted. "What is this? You have set me up? This is why you asked if I'd killed Bettina? You think to get me arrested?"

"No, no, no," Juliette cried. "Never, never, my love, never."

Violet stopped well away from François. "Beatrice, my maid, told me of your meeting. Didn't Juliette send you a note with her? She's a nosy thing, my Beatrice is, but she's brilliant at mending stockings. And we do go through them, don't we, Juliette? Beatrice practically pays her own wages with her needle."

Juliette was gasping, staring at Violet. "What?"

"Juliette would never betray you," Vi told François. "You should trust your wife. I heard her whisper to the inspector how much she loved you. That you were misunderstood. A good man doing his best."

Violet hated the taste of the lies in her mouth, and it

didn't help Juliette either. François kept his wife between himself and Violet. She needed a confession, and she was going to get one for Tomas. Not that she'd attack the man, so why he used his wife as a shield, Violet didn't know.

"Tomas nearly always walks to the folly when he's dealing with his ghosts. Especially at night. You wouldn't know that. Of course it wasn't you who killed Bettina. Bettina was your co-conspirator. Killing her got you nowhere. You'd already moved on. Stealing our things. Fencing them. You *did* meet your fence at the folly, didn't you? I bet you met him near the base on the far side. It's so easy to park an auto on the lane and make your way through the orchard to the folly from that side."

François said nothing, just watched as Violet paced the ballroom. The sheets were thrown over furniture that hadn't been used in decades. A scent of dust hung in the air, making Vi's nose burn.

"What is your point?"

"You saw Charles stab Bettina. Who else would guess where Tomas would go but a good friend? Your golden goose is Charles. What will you tell him? 'Pay up or I'll tell what I know?' Charles would face a noose for that, and he is rather wealthy. But you know that. It's why you threw your wife at Charles. You did your research, unlike Bettina."

"You can't prove any of this," François snarled. "No one will believe a woman's wild guesses. No one. There is evidence that Mary stole those things. Juliette will back me up when I say that you are lying. Two against one. Charles will have to pay more for my inconvenience."

Juliette squeaked when he said her name, and Violet was guessing that she would be walking away bruised. She would, however, be walking away.

"I thought it was you who killed Bettina," Violet said. "I thought for sure that a man who would whore his wife and lie to everyone would be just the kind of person to kill the greedy Bettina."

François snorted. "Death is too final. Blackmail is much more efficient. How fun it will be when no one believes you. I wonder if perhaps you'd also like to agree to pay a small sum. We'll keep this between us and not tell stories so wild your brother will be forced to put you in an asylum."

Violet laughed at that. "If you think Victor would put me in an asylum, you are a fool. Just as you are a fool for thinking that because you complained about Mary, anyone will believe she stole anything. The great niece of the butler who was literally raised in this house versus a lying, conniving criminal? You're going to jail. Jack will find your fence. He'll get a second witness that Charles killed Bettina, and the rest of us will go back to our parties and our nightclubs and our over-sized, yet stuffed, closets. Nothing will change for us. Everything for you. It's how it always works out, isn't it? For the rich like us?"

François snarled as Violet added, "Did you forget the fence?"

"He wasn't there when Charles arrived," François said. "It's still your word against mine and I have a second witness."

"Mmm," Violet said. "Does Charles know that you know? If he's willing to kill a woman he thought he was in love with, what will he do to you? I'm guessing a gunshot. At a distance. He's quite the...what's the word you boys use? Target-hitter?"

"I think," Victor said from the balcony, "the word you are looking for is crack shot, darling. Or marksman. You quite made me turn over in my grave when you hopped up like that."

François gasped in horror. A moment later, he threw his wife at Violet and darted towards the door. Juliette crashed into Violet, knocking them both to the floor. Before he made it more than a few steps, Jack stepped out from behind the curtains. He stuck his foot out, and François tripped with a solid shove to help him down. A second later, the policeman moved to apprehend François.

The look Jack shot Violet was enraged, but she said, "That frees Tomas, doesn't it? It's enough?"

"It's enough," Jack snapped. "We'll be talking later."

He left the ballroom, shouting instructions at the officer holding François.

Victor carefully lifted the weeping Juliette off of Violet and then pulled Vi to her feet.

"How long do you think it'll take for Jack to arrest Charles?" Violet asked.

"He's probably on his way now," Victor said. "We should have known. We were so afraid to see Tomas as the killer, we didn't think long enough about how Charles took Bettina out of the party. About how Charles knew where Tomas would be. Bettina was trying to get back into his good graces. She'd have followed him anywhere. If we weren't blinded by our worries..."

"We didn't want to believe it was any of us," Violet said, hugging the sobbing Juliette. "And because of that, we were fools. It would have been easier for it to be François."

"Well," Denny announced from the other side of the balustrade, looking down on the scene, "I for one think that my Lila needs to spend less time with this dangerous creature. Violet, I must limit your time with my wife to whenever I have plans with my friends. We shall be taking Tomas with us. You too, Juliette. You too. Let's get ready to go. The train leaves in the morning, and I need the stench of betrayal and heartbreak from my nose before I am forced to be solemn."

Lila shook her head at her husband and skipped down the stairs. "You were so brave, darling one. Don't worry. It'll work out in the end."

Violet remembered the look of fury on Jack's face and was unconvinced.

CHAPTER TWENTY-ONE

The train ride back to London was fraught with emotion and an undercurrent almost as suffocating as when they were trying to sort out who the killer had been. Tomas took the fact that Charles murdered Bettina and left him on the hook for the murder as well as could be expected. Which was to say, he'd been hurt, furious and now seemed entirely unaware of what was happening around him until Violet declared, "Enough! Charles was a fiend. It happens."

Tomas snapped a look at Violet. "I...well...it happens?"

Lila giggled at Tomas's baffled expression.

Violet wasn't done, however, with her pronouncements. "We're going back to London. By Jove! We *are* going to have our birthday party. Lila is going to meet adoptive families with me, and then you all are going to Monaco. You're going to sit in the sun, walk, look after my little sister, and—you, Tomas—are going to get better. Don't come back until you stop seeing your ghosts daily. Weekly even."

"It's not that easy, Vi," Tomas said. His mouth was open and he was staring at Violet as though he'd never seen her before.

Victor said cheerily, "What a good idea, you shrew. You know, Vi, I think you'd be an excellent fishwife. Tomas, consider yourself a lucky man. Usually you see the witty, charming Violet. This angry devil is the other version. Welcome to my world."

Tomas looked between the two of them, mouth agape while Lila gasped at the dig.

"Now, now. We cannot have another twin fight, please," she said. "We should all like to stay friends, and we'll be forced to join sides and bandy wits. Let's just have our tea and talk about the weather."

Denny laughed into his box of chocolates. "You know, love. I believe that was the most reasonable thing you've ever said. It is possible that we're maturing into something more than the flibbertigibbets we swore we'd stay."

"The relentless march of time takes us all," Violet sniffed. She glanced out the window and crossed her arms over her chest as though she were furious. It was all a playact, and Violet had no concern that Victor would take her seriously.

Lila took Violet's hand. Vi put a frown on her face but unobtrusively winked at Lila. Tomas didn't need to know that they were deliberately causing a scene. Violet had, after all, told him to never propose again.

Violet turned back towards the window and her journal. She was exhausted. They had seen Charles, François, and the fence arrested. From there, they'd taken Juliette to Lyme and put her on a boat for America. Even after François was arrested, the poor woman had been terrified he'd look for her. So she'd asked to leave out of a port other than London. They'd be buying a ticket in her name for Spain when they reached London. If François truly tracked Juliette, after he left prison, he'd be looking on the wrong continent.

It would be made even more difficult when Juliette changed her name as soon as she arrived in America. She intended to open a dancing school in some place called

Chicago. Violet smiled at the thought. Finally, Juliette was a freed bird.

"Do you have it?" Violet asked Beatrice.

The maid nodded and grinned. "He's going to love it. I think the little thing might be the cutest puppy I have ever seen."

"Yes, well," Violet said, "he did threaten me with one, once. I thought he might want one, and he won't expect more than the recipes and the alcohol."

Beatrice cooed down at the little spaniel lying on the end of Violet's bed, and Violet turned to take the creature in. Lila had come through when she'd found the dog for Victor. It was sporty enough to keep up with Victor should he be inclined to activity and small enough to happily lie at his feet or—knowing Victor—on his lap.

"Yes, my lady." Beatrice kissed the top of the little dog's head as Violet finished dressing for the evening.

Her gown was wine red with the same colour of beading. A dragon had been embroidered onto the fabric with the beading providing dimensions. Violet placed a red, feathered headband around her face, and wore wine red lipstick rather than the usual apple red she preferred.

Her eye makeup was finished. One spritz of perfume and Violet was ready to go.

"You look lovely, my lady," Beatrice said. "Happy birthday."

Violet smiled and kissed the girl's cheek as she stood to leave the room. She walked down the stairs with a puppy resting on her forearm as Jack walked in. He wore a black suit that was cut to his frame, his penetrating gaze turned up to hers. "You like puppies?"

"Oh." Violet grinned down at the little copper-coloured

beauty. "He's for Victor. Trying to out-spoil him is nearly impossible. He really did get me black pearls." She touched the long strand wrapped around her neck.

Jack paused in the taking off of his overcoat and turned with a wide grin. "The dog is Victor's?"

Violet returned his grin and scratched the puppy's ear with a nod. Jack smirked at the dog and then held out his arm. Slowly, Violet put her free hand in his. This was the first she'd seen him since she'd left Kent, and she had been uncertain of what to expect. Somehow things between them were very different and very much the same.

Hargreaves walked ahead, opening the door to where their friends had gathered.

Victor stood and turned, "Happy birth..."

Violet stared at Victor. He, like her, froze to take her in. Matching dark eyes. Matching slender frames. Matching pointed chins. Matching spaniels on forearms.

Their friends burst into laughter as the two of them hugged and exchanged puppies.

"Happy birthday, darling," they said in unison, and Victor handed Violet a cocktail as the music started.

THE END

Hullo, my friends, I have so much gratitude for you reading my books. If you wouldn't mind, I would be so grateful for a review.

The sequel to this book, A Merry Little Murder, is available now.

Christmas 1923

It's the first Christmas without Aunt Agatha and Violet is having a hard time finding the will to be bright or young. Her brother, Victor, is determined to cheer her up, so he arranges a party between friends to brighten their holidays.

When a body is discovered, Detective Inspector Jack Wakefield is on hand. Their romance may be a off-kilter, but he knows them well enough to be sure neither twin killed the victim. So just who killed this person and why? In finding the killer, will Jack and Violet also discover just what the future holds for them?

Order your copy here.

If you enjoy historical mysteries, you may enjoy, *Death by the Book*, the first in a completed series.

Inspired by classic fiction and Miss Buncle's Book. Death by the Book questions what happens when you throw a murder into idyllic small town England.

July 1936

When Georgette Dorothy Marsh's dividends fall along with the banks, she decides to write a book. Her only hope is to bring her account out of overdraft and possibly buy some hens. The problem is that she has so little imagination she uses her neighbors for inspiration.

She little expects anyone to realize what she's done. So when *Chronicles of Harper's Bend* becomes a bestseller, her neighbors are questing to find out just who this "Joe Johns" is and punish him.

Things escalate beyond what anyone would imagine when one of her prominent characters turns up dead. It seems that the fictional end Georgette had written for the character spurred a real-life murder. Now to find the killer before it is discovered who the author is and she becomes the next victim.

Keep on flipping to read the first chapter or order your copy here.

ALSO BY BETH BYERS

THE VIOLET CARLYLE COZY HISTORICAL MYSTERIES

(This series is ongoing.)

Murder & the Heir

Murder at Kennington House

Murder at the Folly

A Merry Little Murder

Murder Among the Roses

Murder in the Shallows

Gin & Murder

Obsidian Murder

Murder at the Ladies Club

Weddings Vows & Murder

A Jazzy Little Murder

Murder by Chocolate

A Friendly Little Murder

Murder by the Sea

Murder On All Hallows

Murder in the Shadows

A Jolly Little Murder

Hijinks & Murder

Love & Murder

A Zestful Little Murder

A Murder Most Odd

Nearly A Murder

A Treasured Little Murder

A Cozy Little Murder

Masked Murderer

Meddlesome Madness: A short story collection

Silver Bells & Murder

Murder at Midnight

A Fabulous Little Murder

Murder on the Boardwalk

THE MYSTERIES OF SEVERINE DUNOIR

The Mystery at the Edge of Madness

The Mysterious Point of Deceit

Mystery in the Darkest Shadow

The Wicked Fringe of Mystery

The Lurid Possibility of Murder

The Uncountable Price of Mystery

The Inexorable Tide of Mystery

THE POISON INK MYSTERIES

(This series is complete.)

Death By the Book

Death Witnessed

Death by Blackmail

Death Misconstrued

Deathly Ever After

Death in the Mirror

A Merry Little Death

Death Between the Pages

Death in the Beginning

A Lonely Little Death

THE 2ND CHANCE DINER MYSTERIES

(This series is complete.)

Spaghetti, Meatballs, & Murder

Cookies & Catastrophe

Poison & Pie

Double Mocha Murder

Cinnamon Rolls & Cyanide

Tea & Temptation

Donuts & Danger

Scones & Scandal

Lemonade & Loathing

Wedding Cake & Woe

Honeymoons & Honeydew

The Pumpkin Problem

THE HETTIE & RO ADVENTURES

cowritten with Bettie Jane

(This series is complete.)

Philanderer Gone

Adventurer Gone

Holiday Gone

Aeronaut Gone

PREVIEW OF DEATH BY THE BOOK

GEORGETTE MARSH

Georgette Dorothy Marsh stared at the statement from her bank with a dawning horror. The dividends had been falling, but this...this wasn't livable. She bit down on the inside of her lip and swallowed frantically. *What was she going to do?* Tears were burning in the back of her eyes, and her heart was racing frantically.

There wasn't enough for—for—anything. Not for cream for her tea or resoling her shoes or firewood for the winter. Georgette glanced out the window, remembered it was spring, and realized that something must be done.

Something, but *what*?

"Miss?" Eunice said from the doorway, "the tea at Mrs. Wilkes is this afternoon. You asked me to remind you."

Georgette nodded, frantically trying to hide her tears from her maid, but the servant had known Georgette since the day of her birth, caring for her from her infancy to the current day.

"What has happened?"

"The...the dividends," Georgette breathed. She didn't have enough air to speak clearly. "The dividends. It's not enough."

Eunice's head cocked as she examined her mistress and then she said, "Something must be done."

"But what?" Georgette asked, biting down on her lip again. *Hard.*

CHARLES AARON

"Uncle?"

Charles Aaron glanced up from the stack of papers on his desk at his nephew some weeks after Georgette Marsh had written her book in a fury of desperation. It was Robert Aaron who had discovered the book, and it was Charles Aaron who would give it life.

Robert had been working at Aaron & Luther Publishing House for a year before Georgette's book appeared in the mail, and he read the slush pile of books that were submitted by new authors before either of the partners stepped in. It was an excellent rewarding work when you found that one book that separated itself from the pile, and Robert got that thrill of excitement every time he found a book that had a touch of *something*. It was the very feeling that had Charles himself pursuing a career in publishing and eventually creating his own firm.

It didn't seem to matter that Charles had his long history of discovering authors and their books. Familiarity had most definitely *not* led to contempt. He was, he had to admit, in love with reading—fiction especially—and the creative mind. He had learned that some of the books he found would speak only to him.

Often, however, some he loved would become best sellers. With the best sellers, Charles felt he was sharing a delightful secret with the world. There was magic in discovering a new writer. A contagious sort of magic that had infected Robert. There was nothing that Charles enjoyed more than hearing someone recommend a book he'd published to another.

"You've found something?"

Robert shrugged, but he also handed the manuscript over a smile right on the edge of his lips and shining eyes that flicked to the manuscript over and over again. "Yes, I think so." He wasn't confident enough yet to feel certain, but Charles had noticed for some time that Robert was getting closer and closer to no longer needing anyone to guide him.

"I'll look it over soon."

It was the end of the day and Charles had a headache building behind his eyes. He always did on the days when he had to deal with the bestseller Thomas Spencer. He was too successful for his own good and expected any publishing company to bend entirely to his will.

Robert watched Charles load the manuscript into his satchel, bouncing just a little before he pulled back and cleared his throat. The boy—man, Charles supposed—smoothed his suit, flashed a grin, and left the office. Leaving for the day wasn't a bad plan. He took his satchel and—as usual—had dinner at his club before retiring to a corner of the room with an overstuffed armchair, an Old-Fashioned, and his pipe.

Charles glanced around the club, noting the other regulars. Most of them were bachelors who found it easier to eat at the club than to employ a cook. Every once in a while there was a family man who'd escaped the house for an evening with the gents, but for the most part—it was bachelors like himself.

When Charles opened the neat pages of 'Joseph Jones's *The Chronicles of Harper's Bend,* he intended to read only a small portion of the book. To get a feel for what Robert had seen and perhaps determine whether it was worth a more thorough look. After a few pages, Charles decided upon just a few more. A few more pages after that, and he left his club to return home and finish the book by his own fire.

It might have been early summer, but they were also in the middle of a ferocious storm. Charles preferred the crackle of fire wherever possible when he read, as well as a good cup of tea. There was no question that the book was well done. There was no question that Charles would be contacting the author and making an offer on the book. *The Chronicles of Harper's Bend* was, in fact, so captivating in its honesty, he couldn't quite decide whether this author loved the small towns of England or despised them. He rather felt it might be both.

Either way, it was quietly sarcastic and so true to the little village that raised Charles Aaron that he felt he might turn the page and discover the old woman who'd lived next door to his parents or the vicar of the church he'd attended as a boy. Charles felt as though he knew the people stepping off the pages.

Yes, Charles thought, yes. This one, he thought, *this* would be a best seller. Charles could feel it in his bones. He tapped out his pipe into the ashtray. This would be one of those books he looked back on with pride at having been the first to know that this book was the next big thing. Despite the lateness of the hour, Charles approached his bedroom with an energized delight. A letter would be going out in the morning.

GEORGETTE MARSH

It was on the very night that Charles read the *Chronicles* that Miss Georgette Dorothy Marsh paced, once again, in front of her fireplace. The wind whipped through the town of Bard's Crook sending a flurry of leaves swirling around the graves in the small churchyard and then shooing them down to a small lane off of High Street where the elderly Mrs.

Henry Parker had been awake for some time. She had woken worried over her granddaughter who was recovering too slowly from the measles.

The wind rushed through the cottages at the end of the lane, causing the gate at the Wilkes house to rattle. Dr. Wilkes and his wife were curled up together in their bed sharing warmth in the face of the changing weather. A couple much in love, snuggling into their beds on a windy evening was a joy for them both.

The leaves settled into a pile in the corner of the picket fence right at the very last cottage on that lane of Miss Georgette Dorothy Marsh. Throughout most of Bard's Crook, people were sleeping. Their hot water bottles were at the ends of their beds, their blankets were piled high, and they went to bed prepared for another day. The unseasonable chill had more than one household enjoying a warm cup of milk at bedtime, though not Miss Marsh's economizing household.

Miss Marsh, unlike the others, was not asleep. She didn't have a fire as she was quite at the end of her income and every adjustment must be made. If she were going to be honest with herself, and she very much didn't want to be—she was past the end of her income. Her account had become overdraft, her dividends had dried up, and it might be time to recognize that her last-ditch effort of writing a book about her neighbors had not been successful.

She had looked at the lives of folks like Anthony Trollope who both worked and wrote novels and Louisa May Alcott who wrote to relieve the stress of her life and to help bring in financial help. As much as Georgette loved to read, and she did, she loved the idea that somewhere out there an author was using their art to restart their lives. There was a romance to being a writer, but she wondered just how many writers were pragmatic behind the fairytales they crafted. It wasn't, Georgette thought, going to be her story like Louisa May Alcott. Georgette was going to do something else.

"Miss Georgie," Eunice said, "I can hear you. You'll catch something dreadful if you don't sleep." The sound of muttering chased Georgie, who had little doubt Eunice was complaining about catching something dreadful herself.

"I'm sorry, Eunice," Georgie called. "I—" Georgie opened the door to her bedroom and faced the woman. She had worked for Mr. and Mrs. Marsh when Georgie had been born and in all the years of loss and change, Eunice had never left Georgie. Even now when the economies made them both uncomfortable. "Perhaps—"

"It'll be all right in the end, Miss Georgie. Now to bed with you."

Georgette did not, however, go to bed. Instead, she pulled out her pen and paper and listed all of the things she might do to further economize. They had a kitchen garden already, and it provided the vast majority of what they ate. They did their own mending and did not buy new clothes. They had one goat that they milked and made their own cheese. Though Georgette had to recognize that she rather feared goats. They were, of all creatures, devils. They would just randomly knock one over.

Georgie shivered and refused to consider further goats. Perhaps she could tutor someone? She thought about those she knew and realized that no one in Bard's Crook would hire the quiet Georgette Dorothy Marsh to influence their children. The village's wallflower and cipher? Hardly a legitimate option for any caring parent. Georgette was all too aware of what her neighbors thought of her. She rose again, pacing more quietly as she considered and rejected her options.

Georgie paced until quite late and then sat down with her pen and paper and wondered if she should try again with her writing. Something else. Something with more imagination. She had started her book with fits until she'd landed on practicing writing by describing an episode of her village. It had grown into something more, something beyond Bard's Crook with just conclusions to the lives she saw around her.

When she'd started *The Chronicles of Harper's Bend,* she had been more desperate than desirous of a career in writing. Once again, she recognized that she must do something and she wasn't well-suited to anything but writing. There were no typist jobs in Bard's Crook, no secretarial work. The time when rich men paid for companions for their wives or elderly mothers was over, and the whole of the world was struggling to survive, Georgette included.

She'd thought of going to London for work, but if she left her snug little cottage, she'd have to pay for lodging elsewhere. Georgie sighed into her palm and then went to bed. There was little else to do at that moment. Something, however, must be done.

Made in United States
Troutdale, OR
09/09/2023